Panth
Caroline's Story
By Christy Perry Tuohey

To a fellow
West Virginian!
I hope you enjoy
Caroline's story!
 Best wishes,
 Christy

Copyright © 2015 by Mountain Mama Press

All Rights Reserved

Library of Congress Control Number 2015917111

ISBN 978-0-9968984-0-9 (print book)

Cover design: Tamera Mams

Author photo: Josh Wells/K&W Photography

For Minnie Velma Backus, 1898-1994

Table of Contents

Prologue

Peters Creek March 3rd, 1854
Miss Caroline Grose
Very Much Respected Miss,

You will please pardon the liberty I have taken in thus addressing you. For I have no excuse to offer, only my ardent love, which I think will be sufficient to plead my pardon. I have for some time had an anxious desire to form a closer acquaintance with you. But dared not make known my wish untill now. Your beauty and amiability have long since attracted my admiration and led me to ardently desire to form a more intimate acquaintance with you.

He paused, let out a breath he had been holding in, and ran his left hand through his hair. His right hand trembled just a little as he dipped his pen into the inkwell on his desk.

And to this end, have written these few lines merely to ask if I may console myself with the hope that I can at some convenient time be favoured with an opportunity of an interview with you....

I subscribe myself yours with assurance of respect,

Nathan Hanna

So silently they slipped away,

We hardly knew just how,

They too abide in brighter day,

To God's command we bow.

From "The Silent Transfer," a poem written by Benjamin Franklin Backus Jr. "by the roadside" at Strouds, West Virginia, July 23, 1900

Chapter One

Listen to me, you who pursue righteousness, you who seek the Lord: look to the rock from which you were hewn, and to the quarry from which you were dug.

– Isaiah 51:1

September 1844

"Preacher's here! Hey, Preacher!" Wesley shouted as he ran out into the yard.

I wiped my hands on my apron and walked to the door. "Shut the door behind you when you run out!" I yelled as crispy leaves blew into the kitchen. Pastor Jonathan Conroy rode up our mountain on his chestnut bay. I smiled and waved as I stepped outside. I was always happy to see our circuit rider, knowing he would bring with him bits of news and penny candy—along with the word of God, of course.

"Hello, lad!" the pastor yelled to my twelve-year-old brother. "What a beautiful fall day it is!" Wesley's first name was Socrates, and like the ancient philosopher for whom he was named, he always had a thousand questions waiting for "Preacher," as we called him. I often had a few questions myself.

"Who did you see in Summersville, Preacher?" I asked. "Were there any—"

He chuckled. "Caroline, my dear, I've scarcely gotten here and there you go with your questions." He smiled at me, pouches beneath his kind blue eyes crinkling like paper sacks.

"Mighty good to see you, Pastor Conroy!" my mother called, carrying a brown crock loaded with potatoes in her petite hands. Her dark hair was skimmed back into a tight bun. She grinned at Preacher. "I think we'll have a good number here tomorrow night."

"That's fine, just fine," he said, unbuckling his pack from the saddle, wisps of white hair sticking out beneath his hat. Preacher's deep voice sounded like dark honey. "God laid a message on my heart as I rode across this beautiful day, Susan. I do believe He has something he wants me to share with the good folks on Panther Mountain."

Panther Mountain was my home in the Virginia hills. Papa called us mountaineers because we lived in the high peaks of Western Virginia. Our farm sat northeast of the Gauley River. The house was layered with clapboards cut from the finest Nicholas County timber. From our front door, you could see the chicken coop and smokehouse across the yard. A little way farther was the cornfield with the barn alongside it. The pigpen was next to the barn. Our cows and horses grazed in the meadow, tails swishing, often bunched up together next to the split-rail fence. Thick forest lined the edge of the meadow and the land beyond our backyard.

I had five brothers and five sisters, and I was born somewhere in the middle, in the year 1825. We all worked hard helping with the crops and the animals. Our land was beautiful, full of maples, birches, elms, and apple trees. As winter turned to spring, maple sap flowed and we had syrup to sweeten our corn pone, johnnycakes, and biscuits, and as the days grew warmer, our cherry grove burst with pink blossoms and sweet fruit.

Preacher Conroy visited us about once a month and stayed at our house. He was the traveling pastor for our district, and he held prayer meetings in the yard or in our living room, depending on the weather. He also led our worship services at Bethel Methodist Episcopal. My parents, aunts and uncles, and neighbors built the church shortly before I was born. The men chopped down trees and laid the squared-off logs for the church house. The women washed and carded wool, spun and dyed the yarn, wove and sewed the cloths for the pulpit and altar.

I wiped my face on my sleeve as I talked to Preacher at the hitching post. It was one of those warm fall days, sun blazing, hills dotted with brilliant oranges, yellows, and reds. My dark hair hung in a braid, and tiny spiral curls of hair clung to my sweaty forehead. I spied my little sister out of the corner of my eye. Jerusha was up to her elbows in mud in the pigpen where she loved to cool off with her porky friends. She didn't mind the flies.

"Rushie, git yourself to the pump and wash up! Mama needs help in the kitchen."

"Caroline, kindly put the kettle over the fire for tea," my mother called out to me from the kitchen door. "Where's your other sister?"

My other sister—I knew which one she was talking about—was probably under the shade tree watching the birds or reading a book or drawing on a slate. Mary Anne was an expert at avoiding the work of the day. I trudged into the house. "Probably up on the hill," I replied.

Jerusha swung through the kitchen door, hands and forearms washed, and cried "I'm hungry!" I handed her a carrot stub to chew on, then poured a pitcher of cold water into the kettle and listened to Mama and Pastor Conroy talk. I sat at the table with them while I cleaned and chopped sassafras root for tea.

"Preacher," I asked, "can you tell me now who you saw in Summersville?"

"Why, of course, Caroline," he said as he turned to me with a wide grin. "Well, let's see, I greeted Brother Fitzwater who was on some errands around town. And I saw the Hannas…."

"The boys?" I bit my lip.

"Yes, the boys and their father. They brought a couple of calves into town to sell. I reminded them about the camp meeting."

My heart was beating faster now. I thought of Nathan and his blue eyes and curly hair.

Mama interrupted my thoughts. "Caroline, please go find your sister and tell her that I need her to help with supper."

"Yes, ma'am." I got up from the table and went outside to look for Mary Anne.

Mama said Mary Anne and I were competitive with one another because we were so close in age. That fall I was almost nineteen; she turned sixteen in May. When I found her, she was leaning on a hay roll under one of the big shade trees down the meadow from the house, legs crossed, reading a book.

"Mama says she needs you to fetch corn and beans for supper," I yelled as I walked up the hill.

"In a minute," she replied, not looking up from her book.

"No, now," I said sharply. She was never in a hurry to do anything, and it frustrated me.

"Well, why don't *you* do it?" she snapped.

"Because I'm doing about ten other things, including rounding up the young'uns and making tea for Preacher and helping with the sewing and—"

"Yes, yes, we all know how hard you're working, Caroline. Why can't you ever just stop and relax?" Mary Anne sat up slowly and gathered up her books.

"Relax? Too much to do around here for that!" I snorted and plodded back down the short hill with Mary Anne lollygagging behind. Papa was at the foot of the hill skinning squirrels on the low branch of a poplar tree. I wrinkled my nose.

"Ya got to take off his shirt first, then take off his pants," Papa said with a smile.

"Hmm..." I frowned.

"You want to eat, don't you?" I winced, watching him strip the fur off the dead squirrel. "Have your brothers come in from the fields yet?"

"Not yet, but Preacher is here and he's having tea with Mama."

"Good, good," said Papa. "All right then. Here, take these so your mother can make stew tonight." Papa handed me a leather pouch full of carcasses.

Mary Anne wound her way down the hill, lazily weaving one foot in front of the other. I strapped the pouch across one shoulder and lugged it past the cornfield. My brother Wesley was pushing a wheelbarrow full of pumpkins down from the field and came my way. Wesley looked like my father, dark-haired, compact, and muscular.

"Preacher's here," I told him, and he nodded.

When we reached the house, the boys set the wheelbarrow down and toted pumpkins to the porch. Mary Anne came up from the root cellar with some ears of corn on top of a basket of string beans. My sister Margaret and Mama were in the kitchen. I dumped the squirrel carcasses into a crock of salt water sitting on the stove.

I washed up outside at the pump and climbed the steps to the porch to shuck corn. Margaret sliced bread and slipped a hunk of salt pork into the pot of pinto beans boiling over the fire. My stomach rumbled. Supper couldn't come soon enough.

***

After we ate, my older brother Franklin stood up from the table and said, "How about a fire outside this evening? We can roast those chestnuts you young'uns gathered."

"Yes! Yes!" my sisters and brothers shouted. I told Mama I'd give the little ones their baths in the kitchen. That way I could listen in as the grownups talked after dinner.

14

Jerusha laughed and splashed so much in the bath that she soaked me and the floor all around the tin tub. Preacher, Papa, and Mama sat around the table after dinner and shared gossip and stories. The general store had gotten a parcel from Richmond that included castor oil, which was a mite dear. Hog prices were down but cattle were up.

And then the talk turned a bit more serious.

"My friends, I have been doing a great deal of reading of late. My brother in ministry, the Reverend Daniel De Vinné of New York, has written words that have pierced my heart."

"What does he write about?" Mama asked.

"He writes that slavery is turning away thousands from our church. He believes it insults the moral sense of hundreds of thousands who otherwise would accept our ministry."

"Well, I can't help but agree with that," Mama said. "You know as well as anyone living here in the mountains that we have no need of holding slaves."

She was right. Western Virginia had no plantations like those in the eastern part of the state. The folks in Nicholas were mostly farmers, blacksmiths, shop owners, and such.

There were a few slave owners in the county. Some were fellow church members, like James Sims. I always wondered what went through his mind as he listened to the scriptures on Sunday mornings, sitting in the sanctuary with his own slaves. Did he just not listen to the passages that dealt with every person's freedom in Christ?

"True, my sister, but too many—even in our own small congregation here—oppose the shackling of human life only for economic reasons," Preacher said. "What Reverend De Vinné is proposing is that we must stand on our Christian Methodist principles against slavery."

"Is this the word you spoke of?" Mama asked. "The word you say the Lord gave to you as you traveled here today?"

Pastor Conroy smiled kindly. "I'm praying on it, Susan. I'm praying on it."

***

Morning came too early for me, as it always did, and I stared at the wood beams above me for some time before peeling off the quilts, swinging my legs out, and touching the cold wood floor with my toes. Mary Anne, Martha, and I shared a room on the second floor. They were still sound asleep.

I washed my face at the basin, combed and braided my hair, and slipped my work apron over my nightclothes.

It was dark out and the house was chilly. Papa had just lit a fresh fire in the kitchen. "Good mornin', darlin'," he greeted me. "You'd best hurry—your brothers and sisters are already out milking."

"Going now," I answered as I pulled on my shawl and picked up the water bucket. Outside, I unlatched the coop and scattered scratch for the hens. Barney the rooster hopped up on the fence and began his wake-up calls to our mountain neighbors. I looked out into the trees through the meadow mist, their branches barely lit by the dimming moon, and saw calm, slender deer slipping through the rhododendron bushes. Behind them, I saw what looked like a stooped figure hobbling,

16

squat, close to the ground, moving from behind one tree to another. I rubbed my eyes—was that real or was I sleepy, still dreaming? Could have been anything. Strange.

I drew a bucket of water from the well and hauled it inside. Mama was in the kitchen, heating last night's corn pone in the fireplace oven. "Good morning, Caroline. Did you sleep all right?"

I nodded. My sister Harriet Jane held Jerusha's hand and stumbled to the table. Wesley joined us in the kitchen, yawning, stretching, and tugging on his suspenders.

"Now you all be sure to put some bread and meat in your sacks," I said over my shoulder. "Hurry up and eat or you'll be late for school. Mary Anne, get up!"

I finished my breakfast and helped the young'uns with their cloth book bags. Martha, Will, Wesley, and Harriet headed down the road to the Backus house for school.

I thought about my school days as I cleared the table. The Backus kitchen always smelled of warm bread and chicken broth. Mr. Backus— Joe Senior—would gather up kitchen chairs and arrange them in two rows near the hearth. There were my brothers and sisters and me, along with the Backus children—Frank, Joe Junior, Isaac, Maggie, and Henry— and some others from the mountain. Henry was the oldest. Frank was next; he was named after Benjamin Franklin, but we never used his full name. Maggie and Joe were the youngest in class.

First thing every morning, we would stand next to our chairs and say together, "Good morning, Teacher."

"Good morning, students!" Joseph Backus was a tall, thin man with watery blue eyes like a Dutchman's and a kind face. He wore wire-rimmed glasses, and his wispy blond hair curled about his ears. He would lead us in our morning prayer, and we could see a small cloth flag hanging from the cupboard as we listened to our American history lessons.

I remembered one day when I was about fourteen, I sat in the grass near a pile of rocks in the side yard at recess, reading Jane Austen's *Pride and Prejudice.* I sucked in a sharp breath as I read Mr. Darcy's admission of love for Elizabeth:

> *In vain have I struggled. It will not do. My feelings will not be repressed. You must allow me to tell you how ardently I admire and love you.*

"Set still, Caroline!" Frank Backus shouted. "Don't move!"

I must have been lost in the words, because I didn't even notice the copperhead that had slithered up right next to me. A rock ricocheted off a big stone next to me, and the snake jerked back, then reared itself into striking position.

Then Frank, who was younger and smaller than me, pushed me away from the stones and heaved a rock the size of a small pumpkin down on top of the snake. He smashed its head.

Margaret ran over and grabbed my trembling hands and helped me up. "Thank you, Jesus! Are you all right?" Everyone stood around, eyes wide. I nodded. "Are you all right, Frank?"

"I think so," said Frank, his face flushed. He wiped his blond hair off his brow and kicked the dead snake off the stone. "I tried to get him with my slingshot, but I'm not that good of an aim."

"Thank you," I said, shaky. Frank picked my book up out of the dirt, closed it, brushed it off, and handed it to me. He was a quiet, bashful boy and looked down at the ground as if he were embarrassed that he had saved me from danger.

***

After supper that night, Preacher stood in our living room in front of the fireplace. The Backuses, Dorseys, and Renicks came, and Suzanne Morris and her family also rode up the mountain to join us. She was my dearest friend, and we could talk about everything together. I gave her a hug as she came through the front door, bending over a bit since I was taller.

The boys brought several log benches in from the yard and dragged them across the living room floor, lining them up for the prayer meeting. When all was ready, we stood up and Preacher spoke the first two lines of "Come, Thou Long-Expected Jesus":

> *Come, thou long expected Jesus,*
>
> *born to set thy people free;*
>
> *from our fears and sins release us,*
>
> *let us find our rest in thee.*

My father hummed the first note, and we sang the words together.

"You may be seated," Preacher said.

"As we plan for our upcoming camp meeting, let us pray for a good turnout and that many souls will be saved. I would also ask you to pray for our Methodist Episcopal brothers in leadership as they consider a very weighty issue at their conference in New York involving clergymen who are slave owners."

I saw John Dorsey shoot a sideways glance at his wife, and she raised her eyebrows. I wondered what they thought of the prayer request. The talk was that, while the Dorseys did not own slaves, they were not against the idea.

As other families were leaving the prayer meeting, Suzanne and I sat in the parlor and talked.

"Father is grumpy lately," she said. "I think this church business has him bothered."

"How so?" I asked.

"He says he doesn't like the church mixing in politics. Says all Methodists should be treated the same, whether they own slaves or not."

"Well, I heard Preacher telling my mama that when the church accepts slavery, it hurts our Christian witness to the world."

"But yet, Mr. Sims is a faithful Christian who brings his slaves to worship. Maybe there is an exception in the church for men like him?"

"It is confusing," I said, shaking my head. "But Preacher says it's not right for humans to own other humans, and with that I cannot disagree."

Suzanne nodded her head in agreement.

That night after everyone left, I set a candlestick on the washstand next to my bed and scooched under the quilts. Preacher had brought me the book I'd ordered: Charles Dickens's *A Christmas Carol*. I rubbed the brown leather cover with my finger and breathed in the scents of the paper and ink, which I imagined smelled like London itself. I tried to read, but thoughts of the camp meeting popped into my tired mind. Who would I see there, I wondered? Would I see *him*?

Chapter Two

September 1844

Camp meetings were great, fun times. There was a lot of preaching for a few days, of course, but also I could visit with my friends. Hundreds of folks traveled from the hills and hollows of Nicholas, Fayette, and Kanawha Counties to hear the sermons and enjoy food and fellowship. We all traveled by wagon or horseback to the Laurel Creek campground near our little church.

We prepared for our fall meeting, packing baskets with sliced ham and cornbread and crocks of butter and apple pies for the church dinner. The older boys forked hay into the wagon, and we hoisted the little ones up onto the soft straw.

Papa took the reins. "Giddyup!" The wooden wagon rumbled down the mountain road. As we passed the shedding trees, Jerusha grabbed at falling leaves, pretending to catch them.

It took us about a half hour to get to the church grounds. Suzanne waved me over as I walked across the campground. She was sitting in the grass, her dark hair glossy in the sun, watching some of the children from our church. I joined her, and we shared the latest gossip while the boys and girls played with stick dolls, dressing them in calico scraps from Suzanne's sewing basket.

"Guess who's here?" Suzanne asked, her brown eyes twinkling.

"I don't know, who?"

"The Hanna boys!" she squeaked and then clapped her hand to her mouth, afraid everyone had heard her.

A tingle went through me. The Hannas were the handsomest boys around those parts. Their family came to Virginia from Ireland, and there was just something about their charm and wit that could make all the girls giggle and swoon. My heart pounded.

"Do you think they remember our names? From last time?" I whispered.

"Don't know, but we can sure remind them, now can't we?" Suzanne leaned toward me and winked.

The wind picked up and leaves swirled around us. I pulled my shawl tighter around me.   Mama walked over and asked us if we could keep the children quiet during the service. "Yes, ma'am," Suzanne said. I looked out over the crowd, trying to spot Nathan's curly copper hair.

Preacher called to everyone to take their seats, and people found spaces on log benches facing the wooden balcony pulpit. Suzanne and I moved closer with the little girls and boys and found a spot off to the side, scratched dead leaves off the grass with a switch and sat down.

Pastor Conroy began his message. He talked about how our church was splitting in two.

"Brothers and sisters," he began, "what unites us? Is it the love of God? Certainly. Is it love for our neighbors? Again, yes. Is it love for our community and country? One would hope so.

"And yet, we face a time in our history as a Christian church like no other time before. We recall the story of the Good Samaritan as we look around us and ask, 'Who is my neighbor?' Is it the man who lives on my road? On my mountain? Is it the man I worship with on a Sunday? And if so, do my neighbor and I believe in the same God? Do we agree on what is good and what is evil? Do we believe in the same Bible?

"For if we believe in the same God, one would have to assume we believe in the Father, Son, and Holy Spirit as the Trinity, unified, three-in-one. God has spoken to us through his word, and the Holy Spirit has written the Holy Bible by inspiring men. And our brother Jesus Christ has lived among us, as one of us, united with us in love. And what does Jesus command us to do in the Gospels? 'Love one another as I have loved thee.'

"But friends, listen! We do not always believe as our neighbors believe. We do not always agree on what is good and what is evil. We here in Nicholas County, Virginia, disagree with some of our neighbors on whether anyone ought to own slaves. Surely we are not all reading the same Bible! For some use our Holy Scriptures to justify their ownership of humans! They say their Bible allows them to worship on Sunday and go back and work their slaves on their farms Monday through Saturday!

"But the God of the Bible freed the people of Israel, didn't he? Moses led them through the water, which God Almighty rolled back to let them pass over. And listen to what Jesus says to us in the book of Luke: 'The Spirit of the Lord is upon me, because he hath anointed me to preach the gospel to the poor; he hath sent me to heal the brokenhearted, to preach deliverance to the captives, and recovering of sight to the blind, to set at liberty them that are bruised.'

"Friends, there is a bishop in the state of Georgia whom our congregation has asked to step down from the pulpit. Why? Because he is a slave owner. And this request, made out of our deep and abiding love for our Creator God and his love for us, is causing a rift. Oh yes, right here in our own church. Our church is divided! Slavery is the axe, cutting us, separating us from each other. But we must be true to our faith, mustn't we? God does not give us a spirit of fear. He does not want to see his children in chains. We are all God's children, light- and dark-skinned alike!"

"Amen!" someone shouted, and several others murmured in agreement. I looked over at Mr. Sims's slave Fanny. She pressed her lips together and bowed her bonneted head.

One of my fondest memories of Bethel Church was listening to Fanny tell Bible stories. She was chocolate brown with warm, hazel eyes and pearly teeth. She showed me and my sisters how to lash small sticks together with twine to form figures, and we made little clothes for them from quilt scraps. She would use the figures to act out Bible stories. My favorite that she told was about Zaccheus, the little man who couldn't see Jesus during a parade so he climbed a tree to rise above the crowd.

"We must *all* be free, *all* of God's children must be free," Preacher shouted. "*That* is what we believe!"

"Amen!" my father shouted from his bench.

"Hold on there, Preacher!" a man's voice screeched. I turned to see Harman Dawes, the town drunk. He wobbled as he stood up, waving his skinny arms to catch his balance. His tanned face, deeply lined, was screwed up in a scowl. He stank of whiskey, and his salt-and-pepper hair stuck up in peaks. "What do you meeeeean Negroes and whites are equal in God's eyes? That ain't right! Damn it, Preacher, what do you meeean?"

The children squealed. Dawes was flapping and swaying next to where we were sitting on the ground, looking like he might keel over right on top of our group. Sally Backus rushed over to us and helped scoop the children up and away from the reeling drunk.

Sally's son Frank ran over and took hold of little hands as we herded the children over to the side of the church at the edge of the meeting area. My heart was beating hard from being so suddenly startled.

"Are you all right?" he asked, putting a hand on my arm.

"Yes, yes…thank you kindly." I nodded and caught my breath.

Some of the men took Dawes by the elbows and guided him away from the seated crowd. It wasn't too unusual for folks to show up tipsy to camp meetings. They were the biggest events in our community, and drew the saved and the unsaved alike. And some people got religion when they sobered up, though with the hardened drinkers it didn't always take.

Mama had been unpacking and setting up the food table when the uproar began. She joined us under the elms.

"Caroline, Suzanne, you did just fine. Thank you, Sally. Thank you, Frank. That old Mr. Dawes has had a few too many. Shameful to show up to camp meeting in that condition!"

Mama and Mrs. Backus took the children over to the johnny house and then to get something to eat. Suzanne and I went over to the food tables to help the women get lunch ready.

26

I looked across the field and saw Mr. McNutt, Mr. Hanna, Mr. Dorsey, and some others gathered in a bunch. McNutt was one of the few slave owners in the county. He was flush-faced, gesturing with his hands as he talked to the other men.

"Genesis! Exodus! Leviticus!" He pounded his right fist on his left palm each time he named a book. "The Bible is full of slave owners. Abraham! So good a man as Abraham! This preacher is cherry-pickin' to suit what he thinks the flock wants to hear!" John Dorsey nodded his head.

"Caroline, I think I see Nathan over yonder, among the birch trees," Suzanne said.

A chill ran up my spine. I thought about the camp meeting this past summer where I'd first met him. He was splitting logs for benches and I was stirring a pot, and when he took a break he walked up to me and asked for a cup of water.

"Beg pardon, ma'am," he said. I looked into his blue eyes and was frozen for what seemed like a long time.

"Might I have some water, if you please? Choppin' wood has me parched." He wiped damp, reddish-brown curls from his forehead.

"Um, yes…yes indeed," I managed to stammer. "Wait right here."

I walked over to the bucket and ladled some cool water into a cup. I walked slowly back to the table, not wanting to trip and make a fool out of myself.

"Much obliged!" he said and took a big gulp. I watched the sweat pour down his neck.

"Well, I reckon I'd better get back to work. Maybe I'll see you later?"

"I don't know...yes, maybe later."

And as the week went on, I did see Nathan again and again at the meeting. We met under a speckled birch each day and ate our lunches together. We talked about everything and nothing. On the last day of meeting, we took a walk through the grove. He ducked behind a tree and crooked his finger at me to follow.

"You sure are pretty, Caroline," he said, reaching for my hand. His eyes twinkled. He leaned toward me and his warm lips touched mine. It happened so quickly, I didn't know what to do. *I shouldn't*, I thought. But I let him kiss me.

My heart pounded hard so hard I was sure I was shaking. His rough hand still holding mine, Nathan said, "Well, I must go home. I hope to see you again, Caroline."

"I'd like to see you again as well," I answered, out of breath and light-headed. And I dreamed about him and his blue eyes many nights after that.

***

Now there he was, talking to some folks under the trees after the sermon was over. I wondered if I should I go over when my work was done and say hello.

Mary Anne walked over from the group, carrying an armload of plates. I stirred the bean pot. "Well, those Hanna boys sure do move fast," she said with a laugh, shaking her head.

28

"What do you mean, move fast?" I asked.

"That curly-headed one over there is wooing the ladies," she said. "Saw him sneakin' a kiss from Nancy Neil, though he didn't think anyone was watching."

Oh. Oh. Kissing somebody? Someone else? Oh.

Then I felt a weight on my chest, a heavy heat. I pressed my hands to my neck to cool it off.

"What's wrong with you?" Mary Anne asked. "You got the vapors?"

"No, just a little warm from standing over this fire," I answered. So I wasn't special. I wasn't the only one. And my time was growing short.

Chapter Three

Winter 1845

Papa drove the horses the better part of an hour through gently falling snow to get us to the general store in Summersville. Mary Anne and I huddled in the back of the wagon. When we got to Hardman's store, I held my frozen fingers over the wood stove. Boards creaked underfoot as I shuffled back and forth in my boots to speed the warming process. The scents of wet leather and fresh-ground coffee filled the store. Papa took a steaming cup from Mrs. Hardman and joined the conversation with the men playing checkers around the potbellied stove.

Jake Miller was whittling a duck call, and his short, shiny knife left shavings on the floor as he talked.

"Heard tell of some trouble at the church," he said.

"I reckon some are talkin'," Papa said.

Isaac Sims picked up a lathe from a hardware shelf and looked it over. He walked over to the group around the stove. He was dark and slender, wearing a straw hat and dusty overalls. "Time to smooth things out, I'd say," he joked, holding the tool up with his right hand. Papa and the other men chuckled.

Isaac knew about troubles. In his younger years, he had been Mr. Sims's slave. He had a wife and children, but they were owned by another family so they couldn't even live together.

Mr. Backus taught us in school about Isaac. He told us that Sims let Isaac buy his freedom. Well-known as a great hunter, Isaac raised the money by shooting deer and selling the skins on his days off from the Sims farm.

Once Isaac raised enough money, Sims signed a contract that set him free, but by Virginia law, free persons of color were not allowed to stay and live in the state. So many people in the county liked Isaac and thought he should be able to stay in the community, they petitioned the Virginia General Assembly. Mr. Backus said he and his father and brothers signed it, and so did Papa's brothers Uncle Jeff and Uncle George. More than two hundred Nicholas residents signed it. Lucky for us all, the lawmakers granted the request. Isaac made a home for himself on Little Elk Creek.

Mary Anne walked over to the piece goods counter and fingered bolts of fabric while Wesley stuck his face into the candy cabinet near the cash register. Mail Pouch crates and cracker boxes added blots of color to the store shelves. A poster hung on a wall near the front door:

> *100 dollars reward. RAN AWAY from me on December 19th, Negro boy Joshua, aged 19, tall with dark chestnut complexion. Face large, sullen look. His boots were new and heavy. I will give $100 if taken and secured and delivered. Dr. G. Wilson, Allegany Co., Md.*

He ran away on my birthday, I thought as my eyes scanned the poster once more. He's my age. How cold the escaped slave must be, probably hiding in the woods somewhere with no food.

31

The stove-side talk continued. "Will, what's going to happen when you have to tell your church friends that you cain't sit with 'em anymore?" Jake asked.

"Well, now, I don't think it will come to that." Papa frowned.

"I don't see how it cain't," Jake replied. "You've got some who's for keepin' their slaves and some who's agin' keepin' 'em, and you all say you're good Christians. Cain't both be right. Cain't both be readin' the same scriptures."

"I heard Dorsey is leavin'," said George Brown.

"I hadn't heard," Papa said, his eyebrows raised. "That would be a right shame. Hate to see that. Bethel wouldn't be the same without John and his family."

"I reckon nobody can stop him," Brown continued. "He come from back east, Albemarle, and brought them ideas and sympathies with him."

Mary Anne broke into my listening. "Caroline, what do you think of these calicos for our next quilt?" she asked as she held up some samples.

"Good...I think they will do just fine," I said.

"Miss Grose, you have a parcel," Mrs. Hardman announced. "I'll fetch it for you."

My book had come just in time for Christmas. It was a group of short stories, and one was by a favorite writer of mine, Edgar Allan Poe.

The men around the stove looked up. "Fancy books for this young lady!" Isaac declared.

"This one's full of mystery," I replied with a smile.

Chapter Four

August 1850

The census taker climbed Panther Mountain on a hot August day and went from house to house, asking questions and writing down names and ages. I looked out the kitchen window and saw my cousin D. O. Kelly walking up the road from my brother Covington's house, in a proper dark suit and carrying a ledger book "Come on in, D. O.," Mama invited as she opened the door for him.

Kelly settled on a parlor couch and began asking questions.

"Susan, shall I write you down as Susan or Susanna?"

"Susan, please."

"And your age, if I may?"

"Yes, you may. I'm fifty-one years of age."

I offered him tea and he thanked me. I walked to the kitchen to get cups and saucers as Mama continued to give the assistant marshal all our names and ages. "Please be sure to make it Caroline, not Carolyn, as it's sometimes mistaken."

"Of course, Susan. And her age?"

"Twenty-four. Twenty-five in December," Mama replied.

Without even looking at his face, I knew his reaction, his expression, what he must be thinking. A twenty-four-year-old woman unmarried?

Still living at home with her parents? What could be wrong with her? She's a spinster, no hope for her.

I was wearing an old gray cotton work dress that morning, so Kelly probably thought even more ill of me. Maybe pitied me. Me in my gathered-waist dress and straight-cut drop sleeves. No lace or ruffles. Just plain. Plain as my dark, braided hair.

My older brothers were married, and so were my sisters Margaret and Martha. Mary Anne and I were still at home, but her prospects were better than mine. She was younger and had promised herself to Henry Backus. They would wed soon enough.

As for me, though, I had considered a few as beaus and been courted by a couple, but none felt right to me. Sam Davis, who became our circuit rider last year, was a kind and earnest man. He asked me to sit with him in our parlor one day and chat, and I had the feeling that he might be sweet on me. Looking at his thin, angular face, hat held in his hands, I simply did not feel the same fire that once burned inside me for Nathan. And anyway, what kind of life does a circuit rider's wife have? He would be more married to his congregants than to me and would be gone weeks, maybe even months at a time, leaving me at home alone with the children. It was not what I wanted, though I admired our preachers for their dedication to God and man.

Oh, I had wanted to marry. Sorely wanted to. There were neighbor boys. Ben Foster and I had grown up together, and he was nice enough. There were a couple of town boys whom I thought to be good-looking. But none could compare to my one true love. And he was married to another.

Nathan had been caught kissing Nancy Neil in the camp meeting grove years ago, and she was the one he made his wife. They lived on his family's property along Peter's Creek, or so I'd heard.

I dreamed of getting married at Bethel, envisioned it many times. Mama would sew me a dress of fine white satin with tiny shell buttons all the way down the back. My sisters would fix my long, dark hair into a bun, and I'd wear Grandma's cameo. There would be white bows on the pews and glowing candles on the altar. Papa would walk me down the aisle to my beloved, soon-to-be husband. All of my brothers and sisters, uncles and aunts, neighbors and friends would be there. All except for Suzanne.

My heart was still heavy six years after our church split. Families were torn over the owning of slaves, which the leaders of our denomination were staunchly against. But some went along with those who believed Christians could be slave owners, and they formed their own Methodist Episcopal Church, South. Suzanne and her mother were heartbroken when her father announced that they would leave our congregation at Bethel. The Dorseys and Dunbars left, too. Though two separate churches formed out of the split, we still shared the sanctuary. We no longer worshipped together but at different times on Sundays. Sometimes we "Northern Methodists," as the others called us, had to wait outside—even in rain and snow—as the "Southern Methodists" held their service. Neighbors did not speak to neighbors as they passed on the way in or out of church. Sometimes Suzanne would catch my eye as she left with her family, and I would nod at her.

My thoughts returned to the present as Mama saw D. O. to the front door and I returned to my darning. My nephew Andy burst into the parlor, eyes wide and dark hair mussed. "Auntie Caroline!"

My brother Franklin and his son moved back home after his wife, Sarah, died. I helped him by looking after Andy, who was barely a toddler when his mama passed. He didn't even remember her. We all did what we could to make sure he felt loved and cared for.

"Auntie Caroline, would you please take me to the cave?" he asked.

"The cave? Walk there on a hot day like today?"

"Yes, please! I want to play pirate on the rocks and find the dragon in the cave!"

"Have you had your lunch and washed up?"

"Yes! I have! Look!" He held his little hands up to my face so I could inspect them.

I smiled at him. "Well, so it looks like you have. Let me finish what I'm doing and I'll fetch your shoes."

Down the road, at the edge of our property, there was a path that led down a short hill and through the woods. At the bottom of the hill was a cave where all of us as children loved to play. There were broad, flat slabs of rock near the mouth of the cave where we made up games and pretend stories. Sometimes a rock would serve as a house or a boat. Other times, the cave was a dragon's lair, and we would take turns pretending to be the fire-breathing beast.

Andy would go to the cave every day if he could. My brother Franklin was often under the weather and quite frail. On his bad days, I would step in and be Andy's exploring partner. I enjoyed the coolness of the forest and cave, especially on a warm summer's day.

I plucked a lantern from a shelf by the front door, took Andy's hand, and we set off. A warm breeze blew across our faces as we walked down the road. The leaves would soon turn. Change was in the air.

As we got to the hill, my nephew ran ahead. "Watch yourself, Andy!" I called. Lifting up my skirt, I picked my way down through the gnarly tree roots and mossy rocks, enjoying the relaxing pine scent that filled the air.

Andy was a pirate again that day, sailing his flat rock ship on the high seas. I listened as he described giant, green sea serpents and pretended to batten down the hatches to prepare for a storm on the horizon. When he grew tired of being a pirate, he wandered into the mouth of the cave. I stooped down, lit the wick on the lantern with a friction light, and followed him.

"Auntie Caroline! I found some pirate treasure!" he yelled.

"Oh my, did you now?" His vivid imagination made me smile.

He held up a cuff—dark, metal, bigger around than my forearm. It looked as if it had been broken off, a piece of a chain still dangling.

I took a sharp breath. "My goodness!"

"Do you suppose this came from a slave ship, Auntie?"

I didn't know how to answer him. My head was swirling with ideas, trying to grasp how such an item could be lying on the floor of our cave. My eyes swept around, and I saw a rock stained with fresh blood. I moved to stand between the rock and Andy so he wouldn't see it.

"Andy, why don't you put that in your ship's hold?" I managed. "Over there, that crevice in the rock."

He smiled and took the cuff, dropped it into a crack between rocks, and dusted off his hands. "It will be safe there from the other pirates!" he proclaimed with a grin.

"Yes, yes, I'm sure it will, dear heart. Now why don't we head back to the house? Oh, and Andy, let's keep your treasure a secret for now. We wouldn't want to give away its location to the pirates."

I prayed silently as we walked back to the house that my little nephew would not say a word about the cuff to anyone.

Chapter Five

There is neither Jew nor Gentile, neither slave nor free, nor is there male and female, for you are all one in Christ Jesus.

– Galatians 3:28

August 1850

At dinner that night, we said grace and dug into ham, biscuits, green beans, and peach cobbler.

"Andy, did you and Aunt Caroline have an adventure today?" Franklin asked.

"Yes, Papa. It was quite fun. I was a pirate and I found some treasure!"

"Did you now? Was it in a treasure chest?"

"No, it was—"

"Andy was such a brave pirate today!" I chimed in. "And remember, dear, how you hid your treasure so that no one would find it?"

"Yes, I mustn't tell anyone where it is!" he said, smiling at me.

My stomach tightened as I thought about the cuff in the cave. I knew from reading *Harper's Magazine* that some sort of organized escape route had been created throughout the South for runaway slaves. It was called the Underground Railroad.

Pastor Davis was at the table with us. It was his usual visiting time on the circuit. "Andy, you must be a very good pirate indeed to have rooted out treasure. Where did you find it?"

"Oh, in the cave, Preacher. We were there today playing and I went in and there it was."

"Andy, I believe I promised you a story tonight. Shall we finish our supper and get right to it?" I asked, forcing a nervous smile.

"Yes, ma'am," he agreed. He washed his last bit of biscuit down with milk and said good night to everyone. He scurried up the hall to the room he shared with his father. I fetched his nightshirt and helped pull it over his head. Tucked in, he asked for an ocean story.

"How about an ocean poem?" I asked. He nodded. I pulled a book of poetry from the shelf in the parlor. "This one is called 'The Ocean's Song.'

"We walked amongst the ruins famed in story

Of Rozel-Tower,

And saw the boundless waters stretch in glory

And heave in power.

"O Ocean vast! We heard thy song with wonder,

Whilst waves marked time.

'Appear, O Truth!' thou sang'st with tone of thunder,

'And shine sublime!

41

"'The world's enslaved and hunted down by beagles,

To despots sold.

Souls of deep thinkers, soar like mighty eagles!

The Right uphold.

"'Be born! arise! o'er the earth and wild waves bounding,

Peoples and suns!

Let darkness vanish; tocsins be resounding,

And flash, ye guns!

"'And you who love no pomps of fog or glamour,

Who fear no shocks,

Brave foam and lightning, hurricane and clamour,—

Exiles: the rocks!'"

Andy was soon asleep. Wesley was in the hall as I closed the door. It was still light out, but the sun was fading.

"I need you to help me with something," I whispered. "Will you go to the cave with me now?"

"What? It's almost night."

"Yes, it's a good time to go there. I'll explain on the way. I'll tell everyone we're taking a short walk before bedtime."

On the road, I explained to Wesley that I suspected there was a runaway slave hiding out in our cave. Because of the bloody rock, I was afraid he or she might be injured and need help. It scared me to go back, but I needed to know if someone was hiding there, if only to keep Andy away from playing at the cave.

"Are you sure it was a leg iron?" he asked.

"I don't know what else it could be."

"You stay here on the road," Wesley said in a low voice, heading down the hill. "I'll hide behind the rocks and wait a spell."

The sun slowly disappeared behind the grove. I paced back and forth, biting my nails. What would we do if we found someone there? Would he hurt us?

I heard cracking and crunching below. Wesley came up through the brush.

"The skeeters are biting, and I don't see anyone," he said. "Maybe we should head back up the road."

***

The next morning, as I splashed water on my face at the basin, I told myself that if we had a runaway on our property, he probably ran during the night and was gone. I had a chance to confirm that on my own because Papa had taken Franklin to the doctor in Summersville. Wesley and Andy went with them. I could use the time to look for signs around the cave.

"Morning, Caroline," Mama called from the kitchen as I came down the stairs. "Will you be helping me put up the corn and apples today?" Heavy glass jars were lined up along the kitchen counter, and Mama was filling the big kettle with buckets of water.

"Yes, I most surely will," I replied, trying to think of an excuse to go down the road. "I believe I'll gather some black walnuts first and then be back to peel fruit, if that's all right?"

"Of course. We could use some walnuts for baking. Preacher will be leaving day after tomorrow, and I want to send him off with a pie."

Mary Anne was at the table, finishing her breakfast. "Have you heard anything from Henry?" I asked her, knowing she was anxious for word from her fiancé, who'd gone to Ohio. Henry Backus was an expert fruit grower. He apprenticed at an orchard in Meigs County, Ohio, and planned to bring new varieties of apples to Nicholas County. "Not for a few days. I'm hoping Papa will bring me a letter from town today."

"Does he say when he's coming back to Virginia?"

"Last time he wrote, he said he would be back before Christmas. Then he'll go to Ohio again early next year and bring back apple seedlings for the orchard. How I miss him!"

I got up from the table, tied on my bonnet, and grabbed a lantern and a basket for the nuts. "I'll be down the road and back directly," I said.

A queasy feeling came over me as I made my way back to the cave. I had to know.

I bent down and entered the cave, waddling in a squat until the rock roof sloped high enough for me to stand up straight. I lifted the lantern and looked around. Sleeping bats clung to the cave roof, and lizards skittered about. A strip of cloth, like a ragged piece ripped from mattress ticking, caught my eye. The edge of it peeked out from under a pile of rocks. I stooped down and removed the top ones. Inside, stalks of goldenrod soaked in a drinking gourd filled with murky creek water. Green and brown husks lay in piles, the leavings from a meal of walnuts and chestnuts.

I carefully replaced the rocks to make it look like no one had disturbed them. As I turned to leave, I saw a brown-skinned man standing at the cave's mouth, his dirty shirt and pants tattered. There he was. My God.

He was startled and staggered backward. "Please!" I cried. "Don't hurt me!"

He darted back toward the cave mouth and scrunched down to clear the low hang of its front. He tripped on a tree root, and as he fell, I saw bloody flesh and muscle beneath the iron cuff cutting into his right ankle. He hit his head on a stump and fell limp to the ground.

Chapter Six

August 1850

Sweat poured down my forehead and into my eyes. I breathed hard as I stared at the man sprawled out, face down, in the dirt and ferns outside the cave. I pulled off my bonnet. My head was swimming. If he came to while I was standing there, he might rise up and attack me because I had discovered him in his hideout. Wesley was the only other one who knew of my suspicions about the runaway slave, but he was in Summersville with Papa, Franklin, and Andy. I didn't know who to call on, where to get help.

The crack of a rifle echoed across the woods. It came from the Backus property across the way. Someone was out hunting. "Hello?" I cried out, my voice weak and airy. Silence. "Hello? Can you help me?"

"Hello?" a man's voice cried out.

"Please, help, near the cave!"

Crunching through leaves and brush below, the hunter's form grew larger. He moved quickly, as a younger man would.

"Caroline?" he called out.

"Yes! Is that you, Frank?"

"Yes, on my way," he called, his steps sounding closer.

Frank climbed up through the rhododendron bushes, rifle held to his shoulder. "Caroline, what has happened? Are you all right?"

"I don't know what to do..." Hot tears spilled, my legs wilted, and I sank down to the ground.

Frank looked down at the man on the ground. "Did he hurt you?" His voice grew louder and tighter.

"No, no, I startled him and he fell. He's knocked out cold."

"You startled him?"

"Yes...I...I was looking in the cave to see if we had a fugitive..."

"Lord God Almighty." We looked down at the man, not moving, leg bleeding. His russet face was scratched and scarred. His rough shirt and ragged pants were stained with mud, blood and grass, his bare feet studded with thorns. "We must get help." Frank was out of breath. "You run, get out of here, before he comes to."

"But he's hurt."

"But you're in danger."

"As are you!" My trembling fingers smoothed wisps of hair off my hot face.

Frank looked around the woods. "Where is your father?"

"He's in town, took Frank to the doctor. Wesley and Andy are with him."

"Who is home?"

"Just Mama, Mary Anne, and Sam."

Frank paused for a moment and rubbed his forehead with his right hand.

"All right...Let's pull him into the cave where at least he won't be seen. I'll get him by the legs. Here, take my pouch and hold it 'neath his head as I pull."

Frank took the man's feet and dragged him to the cave mouth. He slowly pulled the heavy, limp body, and I tried to shield the man's head from further damage with the leather bag. Frank squeezed low and got under the rocky hang, pulling from inside. I followed into the dank dark.

Although I had dropped my lantern inside, the flame still burned. As we got the man fully into the cave, I righted it and we had dim light about us.

"I found nut shells and some goldenrod steeping in crick water," I said.

"Must have tried to doctor himself," he said, wiping his brow. "I'll fetch Pa and Joe and we'll figure out what to do."

We stooped low and stepped out of the cave.

"I'll get some medicine and bandages," I said.

"Do not go back into that cave by yourself," he warned.

I gave him a stern look, but I knew he was right.

I hiked up my skirt, climbed the short hill, and ran up the road to our house. I flung open the kitchen door and went to the cupboard to find a bottle of Dr. Jayne's antiseptic.

"Caroline, what on earth has gotten into you?" Mama asked. "Are you running from a bear?"

"Mama…there's…there's a man in the cave. He's…he's…" I could scarcely breathe as I huffed out the words. "He's hurt. Runaway…slave."

Mama took in a sharp breath. "Oh my Lord, what did he do to you?"

"Nothing…. I…startled him and he fell."

As I reached into the cupboard for first aid supplies, Mary Anne clamped her hand around my wrist. "Don't be foolish!" she hissed. "You are not going back to that cave!" Her blue eyes cut right into me.

Pastor Davis appeared at the kitchen door, dressed in a long travel coat. "Ladies, is everything all right?"

Now someone else knew the secret.

I sat down at the table and told everyone what Andy found, that Wesley and I had gone back to make sure the cave was safe, that I went back this morning to check the cave one more time. I described the cuff, the bloody rock, the deep cut in the man's leg.

"Caroline," Sam said slowly, "where is the man now?"

"In the cave. Frank Backus pulled him in, and I helped. Frank went to get Joe and their pa to come to the cave."

"Can you show me where the cave is?"

"Yes. I want to go back and help."

Mary Anne shook her head and muttered, "Girl doesn't have the sense God gave her."

"That's quite enough, Mary Anne!" Mama snapped. "Pastor, do you think it's right for us to help the man?"

"Susan, I believe it is our Christian duty to help him, especially if he's injured."

Mama nodded. "I will pray for the Lord's will in the matter."

"You must stay here, Susan, you and Mary Anne, and keep the kettle on the fire, please," Sam said.

"Yes, of course," Mama replied.

I gathered up the supplies and set off with Sam toward the cave. We saw the Backuses' horses and wagon at the side of the road.

Frank's father and brother were standing at the mouth of the cave when we approached. "Sam." Joe Senior nodded, pinching the brim of his hat. "We have got ourselves a real predicament here."

"Has the man come to?" Sam asked.

"Just a bit ago. He's a mite unsteady but is sitting up."

Sam and Joe Senior ducked down, and I followed them into the cave, where Frank was holding a canteen to the man's lips.

"Frank, is this gentleman able to speak?" Sam asked.

"He has said a few words."

"Sir, I am a pastor. We are here to help you. What is your name?"

"E-e-e. Edward. Matthews," the man sputtered.

"Edward Matthews, where have you come from?"

"B-B-B-B-ath County, suh."

"All the way from Bath County?" Mr. Backus reared his head back a bit. "That's a mighty long way from here."

Edward nodded and leaned his head back, eyes closed. "M-M-M-Massuh got de pattyrollers affa me. I run hard, climbed dem mountains."

"So you escaped from your owner?"

"Yassuh. Lawd, lawd, suhs, please do not send me back dere!"

"Calm yourself there," Sam said gently, crouching down next to Edward and putting a white hand over the escapee's scarred black one. "Let Miss Caroline doctor you. You have a nasty gash on that leg."

With trembling hands, I dabbed at the wound with a cloth wet with antiseptic. Edward winced and sucked in a sharp breath as I cleaned his leg.

"I'm sorry, sir, I don't mean to hurt you," I said. I knew that infection could cost him that leg if I didn't tend to him.

"So what are we to do now, Preacher?" Joe Senior asked.

"Do you have blankets in your wagon?" Sam asked.

"Yes. Why?"

"If one or two of you can wait with me here until the sun goes down, we can try to tote him up to the Groses' in the wagon. We'll have to keep him covered, of course."

Frank and Joe Junior looked at each other. "I'll stay, Preacher," Frank offered. His brother nodded in agreement.

"Now look here, boys—" Joe Senior began.

"Pa, never you mind. It's like you always taught us," Frank replied.

His father pursed his lips and looked down, his wire spectacles low on his nose. "I am mighty afraid that you will be found out by the sheriff. Then what would we do? Helping runaway slaves is against the law." He looked at them and spat out, "You both could wind up behind bars!"

Sam interrupted. "Joe, I understand your concern. I do. But I believe we can help this man. I know of a way. Can't talk about it now, but I will share it with you shortly. May I ask that you not mention our brother Edward here to anyone else, not even Sally? At least for now?"

Joe Senior nodded, his lips pressed in a tight line. I finished bandaging Edward's leg and covered him with my shawl. "I will stay here also," I announced.

"Caroline, it might be best if you go on back home now," Sam said. "Let the menfolk do this. You can help your mama with supper."

I wanted to help the poor man, but my temples pounded as I considered taking part in the plan to spirit him out of the cave and onto our property. Maybe he could just heal up and move on without our help. Surely if he had made it this far, he could make it to the Ohio River and cross to a free state.

I stuffed bloody bandages into a burlap bag and took my leave from the cave. I needed to get rid of the evidence that I had doctored a runaway slave.

Chapter Seven

August 1850

I dug a hole in back of the house and tossed in the bloody cloths. Just as I tamped down the dirt with my shoes, the wagon rumbled up the road. By then it was late afternoon.

"Ho!" Papa shouted at the team of horses. Wesley helped Franklin and Andy down from the wagon as I rounded the corner of the house.

"What's for supper?" Wesley asked.

"Squirrel stew," I answered, suddenly realizing that in all of the hubbub I had not gathered walnuts for the pies or helped my mother with the preserves.

"Hurrah!" shouted Andy as he ran into the house.

I followed him through the front door and ducked into the kitchen. "Mama, what shall we tell Papa? Poor Edward needs a place to hide."

"Let's bring him in here while the others get ready for supper," she answered. She was a practical woman and fairly calm when there was trouble. "We won't tell your brothers."

"Wesley already knows something," I began.

"Oh dear, who else knows?" Mama's eyebrows pinched together.

"Well, Wesley went with me to the cave last night. Mary Anne found out when I came home for bandages. Joe Backus and Frank and Joe Junior and Preacher, of course..."

"We mustn't let this go any further," she said. "Of course your father has to know if we are to be harboring a runaway slave in our barn."

The barn. I hadn't even thought of where we might hide Edward. But the loft was a good place, and we could pile up the hay in such a way that he could be kept out of sight if anyone was snooping around in the barn. Oh, but how we needed to get him out of there quick.

"Will, could you come in for a minute?" my mother called.

"Yes, my darling, of course!" My father walked into the kitchen, took off his rough leather gloves and slapped them down on the wooden table.

"We have a situation, a very serious situation," she began. "Caroline, maybe you can explain it best." Their faces turned to me. I was trembling. Papa sat down at the table.

I swallowed. "Papa, I found...I mean...I was down at the cave with Andy the other day, and he found something that led me to suspect that someone was hiding out in the cave."

"Hiding out? An Indian?" Papa asked.

"No, more like a slave run from his master," I continued, looking down at the table.

"What in tarnation? A slave? In these parts? You must be mistaken, my girl!"

"No, no, I wish I were, Papa. I found him, sure enough, with an iron on his leg, and when he saw me he ran and fell and hit his head. I called for help, and Frank Backus came right away."

My father listened to the details of our discovery and shook his head back and forth, his dark eyes squinting.

"And where is this man now?" he asked.

"Sam, Frank, and Joe are waiting until dark. They said they would bring him here."

"Here?" He jerked up out of his chair and paced around the kitchen. "I saw state patrollers all over Summersville today. They'll be here soon enough, and then what will we do? They'll find him and I'll go to jail!"

"We could put him up in the hay loft, just for tonight," my mother said. "Sam told Caroline he knows of a way to get the man out of here soon and on his way."

Papa exhaled loudly. "So Sam believes this is the right thing for us to do?"

"He says so," said Mama. "Our Christian duty."

"Well, I reckon he's got the good Lord's ear. Hope he's doing some mighty strong praying, 'cause we are surely going to need it."

***

After supper, I sat on the front porch waiting for the Backuses' wagon to roll up the road. Fireflies glowed off and on over the meadow, and frogs sang over at the pond. Franklin and Andy were up the road at our grandparents' house, to keep my little nephew from seeing or hearing the events that were about to unfold. In the distance, I heard squeaky wooden wheels.

Joe Junior and Frank sat up front, and Sam rode in the back next to a mound of blankets. Cows mooed in the barn. Our sheepdog Daisy ran alongside the wagon, barking and biting at the wheels.

They pulled up to the barn in pitch blackness. Papa met them with a lantern, and they pulled back the covers and helped Edward down from the wagon bed. I brought another lantern, along with a bucket filled with leftover stew and bread.

I handed the bucket up to Joe and climbed the ladder to the loft. Edward was still wearing my shawl around his shoulders. He limped over to a spot and eased himself down. Frank had a blacksmith's tool and began cutting the cuff from the slave's leg.

Sam spoke softly to the men. He knew of a pastor in Ohio who helped slaves escape. There was a woman at Point Pleasant called "Aunt Jenny" who helped hide them on boats on the Ohio River. On the other side at Marietta, Sam's Presbyterian pastor friend guided them to a route north to the Great Lake, where they could cross over into Canada.

"So what we need to do here is get our friend to the Ohio. I know of some folks who would meet us at Morris' Ferry and take him on a salt boat down the New to the Kanawha and then on to the Ohio."

"Meet us? Who's *us*?" Papa asked.

"Well, we ought to talk about that. I should be the one."

"How will you get him past without them seeing something?" Frank asked. "It will take more than blankets and straw to get him safely through."

Sam nodded. "I will pray on that, Brother Backus."

"Sam, do not pray too long," Papa said, his voice rising a bit. "The patrollers are all over Nicholas. They know he's nearby."

I could see Edward's eyes widen in the lantern glow.

Chapter Eight

August 1850

Sam knelt down in the hay next to Edward.

"Edward," he said in a low voice, "I believe I can get you onto a boat. You will have to spend a day or two on it, but when you get to the Ohio River, there will be people waiting on the other side to help you. Are you well enough to make that journey tomorrow?"

"Yessuh." Edward nodded quickly. "Yessuh, I will git on dat boat."

"All right then. We must wait until tomorrow afternoon to get you across the Gauley River and then on to the Kanawha. I will be with you. More importantly, your Heavenly Father will be with you. He will help you."

I had a bottle of Pinkham's tonic in my apron pocket and offered a spoonful to Edward. I hoped it would ease his pain and help him sleep.

"Edward," my father began, "just so that we know, what is your last name?"

"Matthews, suh, Edward Matthews."

"Matthews," Papa repeated. "I knew a Matthews who owned a plantation in Bath County, back when I lived there. Lived along the river. Was he your master?"

"Yessuh, dat's him. Massuh Matthews. I cain't go back dere, suh. I will be sorely beaten. Lawd, how massuh will whale on me."

"Well...I'm sure he has his people looking for you. We must be very careful. Promise us not to leave in the night tonight, but wait until tomorrow when Pastor can get you to the river and on."

"I promise, suh. I will stay here. Thank you all kindly."

"Good. We will let you get some rest now while we make plans for getting you away from here."

Sam interrupted. "Will, might we all pray for our brother here before we go?"

"Of course," my father said.

We held hands—me, Frank, Joe, Papa, Sam, and Edward—and bowed our heads as Sam led us in a prayer. "Father God," he whispered, "we pray for your help here tonight. We ask that you will bless our actions as we try to help this man on his way to freedom."

***

I tucked my Bible under my pillow, as if its mere presence there would help the situation. I could scarcely sleep that night and woke long before the dawn's light.

After getting dressed and doing my morning chores, I joined my parents, Wesley, Mary Anne, and Sam in the parlor. Franklin had taken Andy for a walk to keep him from eavesdropping on the planning in the parlor. Sam pulled out a dog-eared map and laid it on the table. He traced the

New, the Kanawha and the Ohio rivers with his index finger, showing us the route the salt boat would take. Thankfully Sam knew this territory well, from his traveling and preaching in the Nicholas and Fayette circuits.

"Will, would you go with me? If anyone asks about our business, we can honestly say that we are shipping cargo to a pastor friend of mine in Belpre, Ohio. That is the truth. We could leave early this afternoon."

My father agreed, and the two men headed out to the barn. "Maybe Henry can be of some help in Ohio," Mary Anne wondered aloud. But Mama discouraged her from writing to him about Edward, saying too many people knew about our fugitive already. My sister frowned and walked out of the room, leaving only Mama and me there.

"Mama," I asked, "what would you think of me going along with them to help?"

"Why in the *world* would you want to do that, Caroline?"

"Well, it might be good for them to have a woman along. Maybe I could help in some way."

"Dear heart, you would draw more attention to them than they need. Pretty girl like you?"

"I am *not* pretty. I am plain and do not attract *any* man's attention," I blurted out.

Mama reached up and touched my cheek. "My beautiful daughter," she said, smiling. "You have no idea how lovely you are. You mustn't believe that you will never have a beau. A man would be lucky to have a fair, kindhearted, brave soul such as you for a wife."

Tears spilled over my cheeks. I was just so tired, so worried, so empty of energy to do anything but cry.

"Now you listen here. I need your help here at home. Your father and Pastor Sam will know what to do to secret our fugitive away."

I nodded, wiped my face, and hugged my mother. I needed to do something to keep my mind off of the danger my father and Pastor had put themselves in.

***

I was washing dishes early that afternoon when I heard horse hoofs pounding the dirt road up to our house.

"Afternoon, ma'am," I heard a man say, and I ran to the window to see Mama standing on the porch, arms folded. There were three men on horseback, one wearing a Western-style hat. Each had a badge pinned to his jacket and carried both a gun and a whip.

"May I help you?" she asked.

"Well, we were just riding up the mountain here when we happened to encounter some members of your household aways back. A little boy told us that he found something in a nearby cave that may be of interest to us. Y'see, we are hunting a fugitive, a slave run away from his master."

"I see," Mama said in a steady voice. "And what did the boy find?" Andy. It must have been Andy who talked to them.

"What appears to be a shackle, of the type that some owners typically put on their slaves. Would you know anything about this?" he asked, pulling out the cuff and showing it to her.

I clenched my fists, digging my nails into my palms. Papa and Sam were at the barn with Edward. What if the men wanted to search there? I've got to go out there and help, I thought. I walked to the door. "Mama?"

Mama turned to me, eyes icy with fear. "Thank you, dear. I was just explaining to the gentlemen here that I had not seen someone they are looking for, a runaway slave. I'm sure you don't have anything to add to that."

"No," I said. It wasn't really a lie. I had no other information to add to the fact that my mother had indeed not seen Edward, even if I had.

"Mind if we take a look around your property?" the officer asked.

"Help yourself," my mother offered, raising her left arm, palm open. "I trust you will not find anyone."

Just then, Papa and Sam drove the wagon up to the front of the house. There were two barrels in the back of it.

"Howdy," Papa said to the patrollers. "What can I do for you, gentlemen?"

The man in the Western hat tipped the brim at my father, identified himself as Smith, and explained his mission to find the runaway slave. "As you know, sir, anyone found harboring a fugitive slave will have to answer to a judge."

"Of course." My father nodded.

"May I ask what you are toting in those barrels, sir?"

Sam spoke up. "My friend William here is helping me ship supplies to a fellow pastor in Ohio," he said, his deep voice projecting as if from the pulpit. "My brother in the clergy is in need of Bibles and other resources for his church."

The patrollers looked at each other. "Mind if we take a look inside those barrels?" Smith asked.

Sam kept his poker face and chuckled. "Well, that is music to my ears! I would be more than happy to share Bibles with you all, but I could simply get some extras for you from the house. The Grose home is where I stay on my way around our church circuit, and we have a great supply of Bibles and hymnals for our home services here."

Just then, Franklin and Andy came walking up the road. "Grandma!" Andy shouted out. "They are looking for a runaway slave!"

"Yes, my dear. We have heard," my mother called, looking a bit flushed.

The patrollers turned to confer with each other, and then Smith addressed us. "Pastor, it appears you are doing good work here. We will leave you to your missionary journey."

"Much obliged," said Sam.

"Good day to you, gentlemen," my father added.

I held my breath until their horses' swishing tails disappeared down the hill. My mother handed Papa a pack full of food and two canteens. "Godspeed, my love," Mama said softly.

***

Many months later, Sam came to stay with us and told us that he had received word from his friend in Belpre. Edward had arrived in Ohio safely, although obviously cramped, having traveled a two-day journey in a barrel on a boat. We could not know for sure where he traveled from there, but I trusted God had helped him to freedom.

Chapter Nine

January 1854

A small group of us sat in our parlor around the fire, stitching colorful quilt patches and chatting. My sister Margaret cut muslin pieces while her daughter Maggie played with blocks on the floor beside us. Suzanne and I worked red and blue gingham strips into log cabin patterns as snowflakes fell outside.

When Suzanne married David Nutter, she was out from under her father's rules and able to keep company with whomever she chose, secessionist or unionist. She and David joined Bethel Church, and we picked up our friendship right where we'd left off in our younger days. What a comfort it was to have her to talk to once again.

"Ouch!" Suzanne cried out. "Pricked my finger."

"That will surely leave a stain, dear," Margaret remarked about the spot of blood that had soaked into the bit of blue gingham. "Caroline, do you have any starch in the house? *Godey's Lady's Book* recommends putting a thick, wet patch of it on cloth to take out bloodstains."

I put down my quilting and walked to the kitchen to look for a tin of starch. As I searched the cupboard, I heard Margaret asking Suzanne if I had any suitors. Silence.

I had grown accustomed to comments murmured behind my back about my old maid status. I would turn twenty-nine next December and was without any prospect of finding a husband. I had resigned myself to the fact that I would live in my parents' home for the rest of my days.

"I found the starch, dear. Bring your square here to the kitchen and we'll set it right," I said.

Jerusha sat down at the piano and played while we quilted. "What is that tune?" Suzanne asked.

"'I Love Thee, Thou Bright Sunny South,'" she answered.

"Lovely," Margaret said. "What a beautiful South we live in, even in these snowy conditions."

The state of Virginia was going through what my father liked to call "growing pains." Fiery editorials were printed in the Richmond newspapers, criticizing the Northern abolitionists who wanted to end slavery. One editor of the *Daily Dispatch* wrote that the South would be better off ruled by the most tyrannical king of Great Britain than by an "abolitionist despot." Public support of slavery in the eastern part of the state ran high, unlike in our part of Virginia, and that tension was the cause of many a street-corner argument in those days.

Margaret mentioned that we were running low on thread and batting and would need to make a trip into Summersville for those and other supplies. We would soon be ready to put up the quilt frame and begin stitching the pieces together.

"Wesley and I will go into town tomorrow," I said. "Give me your list and I'll pick up what we need at Hardman's."

***

My brother loaded the front of the wagon with tin boxes filled with hot coals that would warm our feet on the trip to Summersville. Bundled in my cape and wool bonnet, hands in my fur muff, I was still chilled to the bone by the time we reached town. I took a cup of tea from Mrs. Hardman and went about the shop with a basket to collect quilting supplies.

Over by the potbellied stove, men were talking, voices sometimes rising. "Blasted New York newspapers!"

"Agreed! The ink-stained wretches believe they know best how everyone else should live. What of the South's right to live as we choose?"

"But what of the Negroes' ability to choose? They would choose freedom, of course!"

A deep, velvety voice interjected, "This nonsense about the oppression of slaves has gotten out of hand. Take a look at our own community. Was not a slave allowed to buy his own freedom and live amongst us? One could hardly call him oppressed."

I looked up from the piece goods counter to see a man in a long dark coat with one boot resting on a small barrel, elbow on his knee. His ruddy face and blue eyes gave away his identity. It was Nathan Hanna himself.

Over the years, I had seen him and his wife and children around town, at camp meetings and such, but had not spoken to him. Despite the years that had passed, he was still handsome. His hair was a thick copper shock with the merest sprinkling of gray at the temples.

He looked away from the group, and his eyes fixed on me. Embarrassed, I looked away and turned back to my shopping. I imagined he had long forgotten me. He murmured something to the men, and one answered.

"Wesley, are you almost finished?" I asked. He nodded as he picked up penny nails.

"Excuse me, ma'am," a man's voice, smooth as silk, asked from behind me. "You look so very familiar. Are you Miss Caroline Grose?" Nathan had walked over to the dry goods where I was standing.

"Why, yes sir, I am. And you are?" I knew full well, of course, who he was, but did not want to appear eager or impolite.

"Nathan Hanna, miss. I recognize you from meeting you many years ago. Please forgive my forwardness."

"Oh, that's all right." I smiled. "Nice to meet you—or see you—again, Mr. Hanna." My cheeks warmed, and I suspected the blush had begun.

He remarked on Summersville's new gas lamps and how the weather had been so unusually cold. He then told me he was in town on errands, not the least of which was business at the county courthouse. His wife had recently died, and he was settling some of her legal affairs.

"I am so sorry to hear that, Mr. Hanna. Please accept my heartfelt condolences," I offered.

"Thank you kindly, Miss Grose. I appreciate your words very much."

I didn't know what to do with the information I had just heard, so I looked down at the store's wood floor to gather my thoughts.

"Do you live around here?" he asked me.

"Panther Mountain. It is quite a slow wagon ride in the snow."

Wesley walked over to let me know he was ready to leave. I thanked Nathan for the conversation. On my way to the cash register, I paused at the apothecary shelf and picked up a bottle of lavender water for my basket.

Chapter Ten

February 1854

Frank Backus drove our new pastor up Panther Mountain on a chilly February afternoon. I saw the wagon coming up our road through the bare, black tree branches. Pastor Robert Brooks had just moved over to our Methodist circuit from Beckley and was holding his first prayer meeting at our house that night.

I was reading by the fire and Papa was whittling, the hearth littered with wood shavings, when the knock came at the front door. Papa motioned the two men into the house as they scraped the mud from their boots on the edge of the porch. I walked over to greet our new minister.

"It's a pleasure to meet you, Reverend Brooks," I said as I smiled and extended my hand.

"Likewise, Miss Grose, I am happy to be here," he said with a tip of his hat and a nod of his head.

"May I fetch you some tea after your long ride?" I asked.

"That would be mighty fine, thank you," he answered.

Frank entered the room, hat in hand, and hung his buckskin coat on the rack by the door.

"I wouldn't mind some hot tea myself, Caroline," he said with a grin, smoothing his blond hair back. He looked older, more sophisticated, with his sandy beard.

"Well of course, my friend." I smiled back at him.

Papa was explaining some of our church history to Pastor Brooks when I brought the teapot and cups into the parlor. Frank took the tray from my hands and set it down on the side table. "Thank you, kind sir," I said. He is always so helpful, I thought.

I sat next to Frank on the couch after serving everyone, and he asked me what I had been reading.

"Poetry," I answered and handed him my copy of *Sonnets from the Portuguese*.

"Elizabeth Barrett Browning, one of my favorites," he said as he leafed through the pages. "'How do I love thee? Let me count the ways,'" he read and then looked up at me. The look in his hazel eyes was so intense, my chest ached. I looked down at the rug.

"I don't believe I've ever shared this with you, but I write poetry myself," Frank continued. "It is cathartic for me to let words flow from brain to pen and paper."

"Oh my, that is lovely," I said, my cheeks hot. "Would you consider allowing me to read some of your poems sometime?"

"Indeed, I will bring one next time we meet," he said with a funny half-smile.

The next time Frank and I met was at church that Sunday. After the service ended, he caught up with me at the door and pressed a folded piece of paper into my hand. His hand on mine was warm and rough. "As you requested," he said and gave me that same intense stare straight in the eyes that had caused me to blush in the parlor earlier that week.

I unfolded the paper as I sat in the back of the wagon on the ride home. My heart pounded as I read the neat, inked words.

Time is an enemy

Yet a friend,

As it begins,

So shall it end.

Time spent in your presence—

Oh, how sweet!

Come closer, you beauty,

Can you feel my heart beat?

Time brings us closer,

I pray it will bend

I long for time with you

Once again

—B.F. Backus

I drew in a sharp breath as I read his signature at the bottom of the page. Was this written for me? I wondered. I felt dizzy as the wagon rocked me back and forth along the rutted road.

Chapter Eleven

March 1854

Suzanne and I sat in the kitchen, digging potato eyes out with paring knives on a cold, dark March afternoon. Wesley came into the kitchen with mail from town.

"Something just for you, Caroline," he said brightly. I wiped potato peelings from my hands and took an envelope from him. "Miss Caroline Grose, Panther Mountain" was written on it in an ornate hand.

"Thank you, Wes. Was my package in at the store as well?"

"Yes, ma'am. Here it is."

I untied the string around the brown paper package and held the familiar light blue magazine next to the table-top lantern. It was the last installment of Dickens's *Bleak House*.

Suzanne put a hand over the magazine. "Aren't you going to open your letter?"

"Of course," I said, nodding my head. "It's probably an invitation to the church tea."

I pulled out what turned out to be, in fact, a letter.

Peters Creek, March 3rd, 1854

Very much respected Miss,

You will please pardon the liberty I have taken in thus addressing you. For I have no excuse to offer, only my ardent love, which I think will be sufficient to plead my pardon.

I have for some time had an anxious desire to form an acquaintance with you. But dared not make my wish known untill now. Your beauty and amiability have long since attracted my admiration and led me to ardently desire to form a more intimate acquaintance with you. And to this end, I have written these few lines, merely, to ask whether I may console myself with the hope that I can at some convenient time be favoured with an opportunity of an interview with you.

I wish you to write a line in return to let me know whether you appreciate my wishes or not. If you have no objection to our forming an acquaintance, please let me know it and you may expect a visit from me soon after the receipt of your letter. Please answer whether it would be favourable or not. If favourable, it shall be duly appreciated by me, if not my best wishes shall still follow you.

I subscribe myself yours with assurance of respect,

Nathan Hanna

"Who is it from?" Suzanne asked.

I shook my head, not really believing what I was reading. "It's from Nathan Hanna. He says he would like to know if I would allow him to call."

"Great day in the morning!" she blurted out. "Nathan Hanna would like to visit you? What will you say, dear girl?"

"I...I cannot even think of it. When last we met in town, he was mourning the loss of his dear wife. I do not think it is proper to spend time with a young widower who is so clearly allowing his grief to guide his emotions."

"Caroline," Suzanne replied, her wise, dark eyes looking straight into mine, "it is very thoughtful of you to consider the poor man's feelings in light of his terrible loss. But wouldn't you agree that a meeting with him might be a pleasant way to pass the time and might perhaps even help take his mind off his pain for a short while?"

I exhaled, realizing I was holding my breath as she spoke. "Dear, you know better than anyone about my strong feelings for him in the past, but those feelings faded after he married."

"*Did* they? Or did you just wish it so?"

I could not answer directly. "I do not see what good can come of this. See here, he is speaking of 'ardent love.' How can the man have an 'ardent love' for a woman he barely even knows? He is definitely writing out of misery and loneliness."

"He does have a fine hand," she said, taking the letter from my hand and turning it over. "Well-schooled, I'd say. Did you know that he is quite a landowner?"

"So I have heard. What say we move on to another topic, shall we?"

Suzanne shook her head. "As you wish, dear friend. I only wonder if you are reacting in haste. Perhaps you may want to mull his request over awhile."

I smiled at her. She knew exactly how I was feeling but also knew me well enough to know that I had tried my best to harden my heart to possibilities for romance, so as not to become disappointed. Life seemed safer that way.

***

After Suzanne left, I walked into the parlor and sat at Mama's writing desk, reading the letter over and over again. What could he mean by "ardent love"? I kept wondering. Does he remember the short time, years ago, when we sat together under the trees at the camp meeting, looking into each other's eyes, chatting away? Was there an ember from that time—that kiss—still glowing somewhere in his heart? Or was I making all of this up and overreacting to his words? A rush, a tingling, washed over me.

Mama walked into the room and sat on the sofa. "You seem troubled, my darling," she said to me. "Have you received some bad news?"

"Quite the contrary, Mama," I answered. "I have received a letter from a gentleman who would like to come calling. But his letter leaves me confused."

"Confused? In what way?"

"He is someone whom I admired many years ago. We met at camp meeting, oh, so long ago now, but he soon after was engaged and married, and I did not see him again until a few weeks ago at

Summersville. Now his wife has died and he expresses an interest in coming to call. His letter indicates he is quite fond of me, but I do not see how he could be. He has not seen me since I was nineteen years old."

"I see." Mama's warm brown eyes were so kind, I felt tears springing up. "Well, perhaps he is remembering a lovely time with you from the past and is hopeful for another pleasant time in conversation?"

"I do not know how to reply. I am unsure how I feel about entertaining a practical stranger. Why would a gentleman like him be interested in a woman my age?"

"What is so wrong with your age?" Mama asked.

"I am, as you well know, dear Mother, quite old. Past my prime and 'round again."

She smiled a bit. "So some may say. But you are a beautiful and godly woman, a treasure for any man. Would there be so much harm in allowing him a brief chat in this very parlor?"

I pressed my cheeks into my hands as I leaned my elbows on the desk. "I suppose not. But what would I wear? What should we talk about?"

"We shall come up with a suitable frock for you, and as for what you shall converse about, there are many topics. You are an avid reader with opinions on today's authors. You might discuss church activities. And if all else fails, talk about the weather."

"Mama, you are my most trusted adviser. I shall write a response, but first I need to get a good night's rest to be truly alert and sure of my decision."

Mama rose, took my hands in hers, and kissed my cheek. "Of course, Caroline. I would expect nothing less from a practical girl such as yourself."

I watched her leave the room and sank back into the chair. *Why, God? I thought. Why is this happening to me now? What is the meaning of it?*

Chapter Twelve

March 1854

"Sit still, Caroline, you're making it impossible for me to pin this up straight." My sister Martha was helping me get ready for Nathan's visit, and it was all I could do to keep from leaping out of the chair as she brushed, pulled, rolled, and curled my hair. She had washed it with a mixture of olive oil, rosewater, and soap shavings, and after a period of drying insisted I brush a hundred strokes before she styled it. Because my hair was waist length, this entire process took hours, and I grew nervous that she would still be knotting and pinning even after my gentleman caller arrived.

Then the task of my dressing commenced. I was not used to such a fuss, but of course wanted to look presentable. The corset tightening left me short of breath. Martha and Mama helped me get the crinolines and dress over my head without destroying my sister's handiwork. I balked at wearing a bonnet. I would not have gone through the pains of hairdressing had I thought I would be covering it all up with a hat.

I pinned a floral mosaic brooch to the neckline. Examining myself in the mirror at my dressing table, I saw that the blue and green plaid dress I had chosen at the dressmaker's served me well. The greens accented my dark hair and eyes in a pleasing way. I spied a gray strand of hair and plucked it out. After dabbing my wrists with lavender water, I was ready.

I paced in my room as I waited for my guest's arrival. My head was a jumble of thoughts and worries and occasional resignations to the fact that I was an old maid and if Nathan saw me in the afternoon light of our parlor, he would surely realize that fact. What could a short visit hurt? I would be no worse for the experience, or at least I hoped I would not.

My biggest concern about meeting him was what Papa had told me about some members of the Hanna family. He said that certain of them were supporters of Southern secession. It troubled me to think about Nathan's comments at the store about slaves. He seemed to think that not all slaves were poorly treated. Did he also support a divided United States? I told myself not to make a hasty judgment and prayed for patience and calm as I waited for his arrival.

The knock came and Papa answered the door. My sister Harriet came to my room and let me know that Mr. Hanna had arrived. I wiped my palms on my skirt and headed down the stairs.

There in the parlor stood Nathan and Wesley, my designated chaperone for the visit. The two men were chatting about hunting and fishing when I entered the room. Nathan was wearing a black frock coat with wide lapels, a satin vest and cravat, topped off with a coachman hat, which he removed when I came in.

"Good day, Miss Grose," he said in his velvety voice as he bowed his head. "Lovely to see you again. Thank you for allowing me to call."

"Good day, Mr. Hanna," I replied. "You are most welcome. Please, have a seat."

He sat on one parlor couch, and I sat on the opposite one so that we faced each other in front of the fireplace. He held his hat and gloves, scanning the room with his piercing blue eyes.

Except for some lines in his forehead and crow's feet about the eyes, he looked much the same as in the days when we first met. His wavy hair was combed back from his forehead. A reddish-gray beard, neatly trimmed, edged his strong jaw.

"May I say you're looking well, madam. How do you maintain such a youthful appearance?"

I smiled and blushed. "Oh my...well, that's kind of you to say. I suppose my happy life here on Panther Mountain helps keep me feeling young anyway."

"It certainly suits you." He smiled back, eyes twinkling. We continued our polite chat while Wesley sat in the corner reading, pretending he was not listening. I asked Nathan about his land, where he said he raised cattle and tended to his orchards. He said he was considering selling part of his timberland to an out-of-state investor.

"As I mentioned to you in my letter, I am so very sorry to hear of your wife's passing. Has it been some time now?" I asked.

"A year ago next week," he replied, nodding. "Thank you for your concern. It has been a difficult time, no question. My two daughters and my son have tried their best to carry on, but it is of course a great loss for us."

"Of course it is. Please know that you and your family will remain in my prayers."

"You are very kind, Miss Grose. I appreciate your allowing me to come calling. Sundays can be very lonely days."

Because he had traveled some distance, I offered him a cup of tea. I knew there was a pot on and excused myself to the kitchen.

As we sipped our tea, Nathan commented on the great number of books in our library. "The Grose family is undoubtedly well read," he said.

"We all are fond of books and read whenever possible," I said. "One learns so much about the outer world through books."

"Have you any to recommend? I confess to being quite a slow reader and do not often take the time to sit down and enjoy a good book."

I saw a chance to test his views when he asked this. I walked over to the bookshelf and pulled out *Uncle Tom's Cabin*. "This is quite a good one, very well written. Miss Harriet Stowe has taken the major moral issue of our time—slavery—and delivered quite a sharp critique of the institution."

"Yes, I have heard of this one," Nathan said as he thumbed through the pages. "Quite a controversial novel, from what I understand."

"Indeed, but what some call controversy, I would describe as a bright light illuminating the darkness."

"Miss Grose, you have a fine mind," he said, grinning at me. "Another reason to admire you."

I turned back toward my seat to hide my flushed cheeks and picked up a fan from the end table next to the sofa. I was glad to find something I could hide behind until I regained my composure.

Nathan sat down and finished his tea. "Well, I am afraid it is time for me to go now. I have truly enjoyed our time together today. May I be so bold as to ask if I may call again next Sunday afternoon?"

"Oh, well, let me think a moment. Wesley, do you know of any events we are committed to other than church a week from today?" My brother shook his head.

"Well, if you wish, you may come to call, Mr. Hanna. Next Sunday afternoon."

"I would be honored," he answered with a bow.

Chapter Thirteen

March 19, 1854

A surprise snow kept many of Bethel's worshippers away from the pews that Sunday, but Papa was delivering the sermon, so most of our family was in attendance, and so were many of our neighbors and friends. We left our farms earlier than usual in the event cold and ice slowed the horses in getting us to church on time.

My father was what was known in those days as a licensed exhorter. The title gave him authority in the eyes of the church to lead worship services in the absence of a circuit rider or permanent pastor. He was a gifted speaker and very knowledgeable about the Holy Scriptures. Some friends and family had, over the years, encouraged him to attend seminary and earn a pastoral degree, but he preferred to minister to our church community as a layman. He was but a farmer, he would humbly say, and blessed to serve Bethel Church simply as one of many of God's faithful workers.

We shook snowflakes from our capes, coats, and bonnets and entered the tiny sanctuary. Jerusha played the piano and led us all in hymn singing.

Come, thou Almighty King,

Help us thy name to sing,

Help us to praise:

Father all-glorious,

O'er all victorious,

Come, and reign over us,

Ancient of days.

Papa delivered a meaningful message, as usual, explaining Christ's Sermon on the Mount in a way I had never heard before.

As the service ended that morning, Frank Backus came over to our pew. "Caroline," he said. "How have you been?"

"Very well, thank you, Frank. And you?"

"Good, good. Itching to get this snow out of the way and begin planting." His cocoa-brown coat showed off his broad shoulders.

"I hear Henry is keeping a crowd of apple seedlings in the barn until the ground warms," I said.

"You sisters do talk, I see." He grinned. "Mary Anne and I were discussing the news the other day of your Sunday visitor." I was surprised, and it must have shown on my face. "Not to worry, we were not speaking ill of you."

"Well, I should hope not," I retorted with a little laugh. "And what, pray tell, did you two have to say about the company I kept this past Sunday?"

"Mary Anne mentioned that your visitor was Hanna from Peter's Creek."

"Why, yes. Had I known my social life was a topic of conversation, my ears should have been burning," I said, a bit taken aback.

"I did not mean to give the impression that I have been gossiping about you, Caroline. I wholeheartedly apologize," he said, looking down. "But you must go now, as you are expecting a caller."

"Yes, I must. I will see you in church Sunday next, Frank," I said as I tied on my bonnet. I found it curious that he knew so much about my comings and goings.

Back at home, I ate a bit of bread and not much else at lunch, then retired to my room to write in my journal while waiting for Nathan to arrive. It was the only place I could confess how much I looked forward to Nathan's visit.

Sunday, March 19

Nathan will be calling today and I expect we will get to know each other even better this afternoon than we did last. I am anxious to find out about his personal world and political views, though, and in that anxiousness stirs a bit of dread. I am so very concerned that he may see the world differently than I do. I suppose I am rushing a bit toward thinking of us as a couple, which really I dare not do. As we sat in the parlor last time, I felt the heat of the tiniest hot ember that once burned inside me. Will today's visit stoke that ember? I must control my thoughts and protect my heart.

Harriet appeared at my door. "Caroline, your gentleman caller is here."

My younger sister would act as chaperone this afternoon, as Wesley and the others were out sleigh riding. The parlor fire warmed my face as I walked in to find Nathan waiting for me.

"Madam!" He bowed and smiled at me. "The chilly winds blew me here. You are quite the sight for sore eyes. How are you today?"

"Quite well, thank you, sir." I nodded and pantomimed a curtsy. "It is very nice to see you again." I cautioned myself to remain calm and appear nonchalant even though gazing at his fine face nearly took my breath.

"I brought along a book for you today. Considering your positive review of Harriet Stowe's book, I thought you might like to read one that shows another side of plantation life."

We sat down next to each other on the loveseat. He handed me the book. "*Aunt Phillis's Cabin*," I read aloud. "I am familiar with this genre. Plantation fiction is what they call it, I believe."

"Is that what they call it?" he asked, smiling. "I look forward to hearing your opinion of it."

"I must ask you, Nathan, as you have opened the subject, what are your views of plantation life and, in particular, slavery?"

"Oh, well…. I know not of plantation life as it exists down East," he began. "I do believe that much of the talk I hear from the Northern abolitionists goes against the rights of the Southern man to freely choose to live and work as he pleases."

"But would you not agree that the ownership of humans, not to mention the ill-treatment of those humans, goes against one's Christian beliefs?" I could sense the direction the conversation was taking, and I didn't like it.

"To be sure, there are slaves who have been treated poorly, as we have read in the newspapers. But I also suspect there are quite a number of Negroes who are lucky to be in their state, putting in a hard day's work, enjoying a place to sleep and a meal a day as a reward for their efforts. Do you not agree?"

My heart pounded. All I could see at that moment was Edward's panicked, bloodshot eyes and his wounded leg. *Calm yourself, Caroline. Use reason, not emotion, as best you can.*

"I cannot, unfortunately, agree that anyone could be 'lucky' who does not enjoy freedom, regardless of food or bed offered. It goes against my deep belief that God intends for all of his children to live in freedom."

"Oh dear, I'm afraid we have gotten off on a bad foot with this topic. Please be assured, my dear lady, that I believe we can come to a mutual understanding based on our affection for one another." He stared at me very intently as he spoke. "The love of a good woman has softened the heart of many a rascal such as myself."

Love? Does he presume? I have not said this, I have not shown my heart to him.

"Nathan, I...I don't know what to say. You are using a word that is loaded with power and indicates strong feelings that have not yet been expressed between us." My heart and head were pounding.

"Dearest Caroline, have you not guessed by now that I love you? If not, I apologize for not sooner showing you my truest intentions." He reached over and put his hand on mine. My heart pounded so hard I was sure he could hear it. Harriet looked up from her book, wide-eyed.

"And yet, dear sir, we scarcely know each other. My fear is that we may be worlds apart in our views of life and love, indeed even our spiritual beliefs."

"Please, let me prove my love to you. I will be willing to listen to your views, and I promise to hold them in the utmost regard. Caroline, I would be delighted and honored to hear you say you love me, too."

I looked down at the parlor rug and strained to find words, any words. As I cherished in my heart the thought of this dashing man professing his love to me, something shattered inside me.

"Nathan, thank you so much for your kind words. I feel as though I may have a headache coming on, probably from the change in the weather. Would you please excuse me? Perhaps we might take up this discussion another day."

His brow creased, his eyes searching mine so intently I had to look away. "Of course. I am so sorry to know you're feeling ill. I will take my leave now. Please know you have my best wishes for a quick recovery. I will write soon and hope you will write back to me. Would you do that, Caroline?"

"Yes, yes, of course. Thank you for the visit, Nathan."

We walked to the parlor door. He suddenly, impetuously, put his hand on my cheek, his eyes twinkling as they did on that day long ago in the birch grove. His moustache felt like bristle on my upper lip as he stole a kiss. I pulled back, afraid for Harriet to witness such a brash move. My cheeks were hot as I looked at his face, half-smiling. "Forgive me," he said. "Your beauty has once again carried me away." He put a hand over his heart and bowed. "Good-bye, my dear."

Harriet showed him the door, and I hurried up the stairs to my room.

Chapter Fourteen

March 19, 1854

Tears dripped into my ears as I lay on my bed looking at the ceiling. I was flattened, literally and figuratively. A man I deeply desired had just shown me he may not be the sort of man I wanted as a husband. Or was I being silly, overreacting as I often did? I had waited many years for a partner whom I could truly love and respect. He was the only man I had ever really loved. Or thought I loved.

There was a knock at my bedroom door. It was Harriet. "May I come in?"

"Just a minute," I answered and reached for my handkerchief.

She waited a moment then opened the door a crack. "You have another caller. It's Frank Backus. Should I tell him you are ill?"

"Frank? No, that's all right, Harriet. If it's just Frank, you may tell him to stay. Please ask him to give me a minute and I will be down to see what he wants."

This was rare. I had gone weeks without seeing Frank since he began managing his family's farm. Now I was seeing him twice in one day.

I dried my eyes, blew my nose, smoothed out my dress, and walked downstairs.

Frank sat reading his Bible on one of the sofas in the parlor. He wore his gray wool Sunday coat and string tie. He stood up as I walked into the room.

"Caroline, please forgive me for calling unannounced. I would just like to have a few words with you, if you don't mind. I won't take up much of your time."

"Of course, Frank," I said. "Have a seat." I sat down next to him.

He smoothed the brim of his hat with his fingers as he spoke.

"I hope I am not intruding. I know you are expecting a guest this afternoon," he said.

"No, no, he has come and gone. What is on your mind?"

"I was wondering if you have gotten to know Hanna better now that he has visited a second time?"

"I know that he owns cows and timberland and that he is a slow reader," I replied.

"Well, that may all be true, indeed. Did you also know that he is on the side of the secessionists?"

"No, I had not heard that he himself was such. I was told he may have family who are. He has not said so directly."

"I heard tell that he has been outspoken many times in town about his support of slavery. I was not sure if he had yet shared that with you."

94

"Not exactly. In fact, I recommended he read *Uncle Tom's Cabin*. I imagine he might have reacted more strongly to my suggestion were he genuinely on the secessionist bandwagon."

"Well, all I know is what I have heard," Frank said. "I don't mean to pry." His greenish-brown eyes were swimming with something that I didn't quite understand.

"Frank Backus, why all the sudden concern over whom I am spending time with?"

He looked surprised. "Caroline, it is the world's worst-kept secret that I have long hoped to call on you as more than a friend."

"Why, what has kept you from telling me this secret?" Perhaps he was joshing.

"I thought it was obvious and that perhaps others may have told you. I tried to let you know my feelings through the poem I gave you. I have not been brave enough, I confess, until now. Until I knew I might have a rival."

The thought of the poem he pressed into my hand after church made my cheeks flush.

"I wouldn't put it that way, Frank. One would not say that Mr. Hanna and I are courting."

"I would," he argued.

"Frank, are you teasing me?"

His raised eyebrow indicated he was not. He straightened his tie.

I just could not piece together the words that were suddenly coming out of his mouth. Here he was, someone I had known since childhood, suddenly expressing an interest in me. My heavens, I was six years old when he was born. I remembered him as just a little boy.

"Well...em...this comes as quite a shock," I stammered. "I had not thought of us in that way."

"I understand, Caroline. Really I do. I just ask that you give the idea some time and thought. I would be most honored to call you my own."

"Glory be, you certainly wear your heart on your sleeve now, don't you? I will give this some thought, but please understand that I will continue to receive Nathan as a visitor until I determine where our courtship...friendship...whatever it may be...stands."

"Of course, I would expect you to find that out for yourself. You are a person of great integrity and honesty, and nothing short of the absolute truth would be good enough for you."

He stood up and gave me a nod. "I hope you will consider allowing me to call on you again in the future."

I nodded back, confused but at the same time trying to be polite and friendly.

"I'll see myself to the door. I know well its location." He winked.

"Good-bye, Frank. Be well," I said.

Chapter Fifteen

April 1854

"All the way around and halfway back, the ladies in the lead and the gents in back...."

I had not intended to go to the square dance in town, but Harriet and Wesley were keen on seeing their sweethearts and, as winter had broken and warm spring breezes were blowing, I agreed to chaperone them. As we rode up to the Raders' barn, I could hear a fiddler sawing away at "Sailor's Hornpipe." Inside, kerosene lamps hung from the rafters, brightly lighting the dancers as they linked arms and skirts swirled.

It had been two weeks since I last received a letter from Nathan, and I was fairly certain he did not think much of dances based on what he had written.

Dearest Caroline,

> *How I long to hear from you. Your letters leave me still unsure about your feelings for me and yet I remain very much in love with you. I ardently wish to see you again. News of a square dance in Summersville in April has reached us here in Peters Creek. Though I ordinarily would not care for such an occasion, as I am accused of having two left feet on the dance floor, I would gladly meet you there to gaze upon your beauty once again. Please favor me with a reply as to whether you might be in attendance that night.*

I did not reply to his letter. I felt the need for some distance from him.

My misgivings about Nathan had only increased after I read the book he gave me. *Aunt Phillis's Cabin* was the worst type of Southern literary pap. Author Mary Eastman's assertion that Northerners might, after defeating slavery in the courts, travel south to capture and enslave freed Negroes for themselves, was ludicrous. I could not, in good conscience, give the book a positive review when Nathan asked about my thoughts.

Though we had not seen each other in a month, we exchanged a few letters. As I feared would happen, he continued to defend the "rights of the Southern man" when such topics arose in our letters. And though he always assured me that he truly listened to my ideas, despite their similarity to those of "Northern abolitionists," I did not feel in my heart that he took them into consideration at all. As much as I wanted to believe him, his romantic notion that his affection for me would overcome any differences between us rang hollow.

"Grab your partner, give her a swing, promenade around that ring, take a little walk with that pretty little thing...."

As I watched Wesley and his lady friend cross arms and skip about, I caught sight of a familiar pair of intense blue eyes on the dance floor. Mr. Nathan Hanna, as it turned out, was not sitting at home or even in a corner of the room in fear of embarrassing himself with his "two left feet." He was promenading with a young, dark-haired lady whom I did not recognize. And as the dance ended, he bowed and took her by the hand back to a pair of chairs where, heads bowed close together, they engaged in conversation.

Although I was awash with jealousy, I straightened my back, pulled back my shoulders, and stuck out my chin. So this is the way it would be. If I did not soon return his affections, the lonely widower would move on to his next prospect and perhaps was doing so in front of my eyes.

Frank appeared before me, bowed, and smiled. "Good evening, Caroline. I am delighted to see that you have come to dance."

"Dance? Oh, no, I am simply here to chaperone Wesley and Harriet, not to dance." I managed a smile as the corners of my mouth quivered.

He was clean-shaven, and his sandy hair was smoothed back with scented pomade. His light eyes sparkled. He seemed amused by my wooden response. "Oh, I see. Could I convince you to honor a friend with a turn on the floor? Please?" He held out his hand.

"Oh, I...."

"For a lifelong friend?"

I tilted my head and could not help but grin. "Of course, dear friend," I said and took his warm, rough hand.

As I sashayed in my plaid dress, the skirt of which was so puffed out with crinolines that I must have resembled a hopping mushroom, I smiled and laughed and clapped hands with my friend Frank. It was exhilarating to dance; it freed my mind of heavy thoughts.

When the music stopped and we were quite out of breath, Frank escorted me to a chair and then fetched me a cup of punch. Surely and swiftly, Nathan appeared and got down on one knee to greet me.

"My dearest! Because I did not hear from you, I did not expect you to be in attendance this night," he exclaimed. "Had I known you were coming, I would happily have escorted you."

"No need to apologize, Nathan," I answered, still breathing hard from the dance. "I see you have found a dance partner, and that is as it should be, considering I did not send a reply."

"But I barely know her! Please do not mistake that dance as a sign that I have eyes for another. May it never be!"

Frank returned with punch cups in hand. He tilted his head back and eyed Nathan warily. "Greetings...Hanna, is it?"

Nathan stood up. "Yes, sir. And you are?"

"Frank Backus. A friend of Miss Grose. How do you do?"

"Just fine, thank you, sir. I was just explaining to the lovely Miss Grose that I would have liked to squire her to this evening's dance but did not know she had interest in being here."

"I see. Well, Caroline tells me she is here out of duty to her younger brother and sister, as they needed a chaperone for the evening."

"Ah, of course. Selfless as always. And yet you have taken a turn with the beautiful chaperone, I see. The Virginia reel. What a spirited dance."

Frank and I looked at each other, neither of us knowing quite how to extend the conversation further. Nathan gave me an awkward glance and a dimpled half-smile.

"Well, I must go now. It would be rude to abandon my dance partner. Caroline, may I ask that you favor me with a letter very soon?"

"I will write."

Frank took a seat next to mine and sipped his punch. He stared across the empty dance floor. "He is a persistent suitor. But I am even more persistent and have youthful energy on my side as well," he mused.

"Frank, I…." I wanted to tell him that the letter I intended on writing to Nathan would be one of farewell, but I couldn't form the right words. "Thank you. I had such a nice time dancing with you."

***

The next morning, I sat at my writing desk and prayed: "Father God, please give me the right words to say and guide me in making the right decision."

With an ache in the middle of my chest, I poured my thoughts out in ink.

Dearest Nathan,

> *What a surprise to see you in town last night. I hope you had an enjoyable time and made it safely home, despite the spring rain and muddy roads.*

> *I hope you know that I have enjoyed our visits in the past two months. It was especially kind of you to bring me a book. However, you and I stand worlds apart on important issues that affect us here in Virginia and across the other states. I am unapologetically opposed to slavery and do not believe that any true Christian can, in clear conscience, own another human being. This is simply who I am and this belief has guided me and my family for decades. Though you have said our affection for*

one another will overcome any differences between us, I cannot foresee, as Virgil wrote, "love conquering all" in this case.

With this realization, Nathan, I bid you a very fond farewell. I assure you that I care deeply for you and your family's welfare and will always cherish the time we spent together. But I cannot continue our courtship knowing that we are of two vastly different minds and hearts. My best wishes go with you always.

Fondly,

Caroline

Although a tear or two splashed the paper as I was writing, they fell short of my pen strokes and did not smear my words.

Chapter Sixteen

June 1854

June bugs rasped and crickets chirped a warm summer symphony. Frank held my hand as we sat on the front porch of my house. Although I thought my heart would break after turning Nathan away, I had slowly warmed to Frank's patient courting. I was somewhat embarrassed by our age difference, although Frank did not seem bothered by it in the least. People do not speak kindly of spinsters who "chase" younger men. I could just imagine what the talk at church would be when word spread that we were officially courting. Even godly people could not resist gossip.

Most surprising to me, though, was how I came to truly admire Frank. The boy who had saved me from the snake at recess and helped me drag a runaway slave to safety had grown up into a fine, handsome man.

Though we had known each other since childhood, I wanted to know him better as my feelings for him grew deeper.

"I've been wondering for some time now, why did your father and his brothers change the family name from Backhouse to Backus?" I asked him.

"Well, they tired of folks teasing them," he said. "You know, Backhouse sounds a bit like outhouse or johnny house. It seemed easier to them to change it."

"I understand. People can be so thoughtless with their teasing."

103

"Backus is a pretty good name, don't you think?"

"Of course I do. It is a noble name, dating back centuries to England and Germany from what I understand."

"Do you like the name well enough to make it yours?"

"What are you asking me, Frank Backus?"

"I am asking you if you would consider having me as your husband."

A chill spread through me. I was not completely surprised that he asked me to marry him. We had talked about a future together, and we were very compatible. When he said the words, I hesitated. But only for a moment.

"Yes."

He smiled and kissed my hand, then leaned in. It was a good, long kiss.

Chapter Seventeen

January 1855

We were married on New Year's Day. Glorious, whirling snowflakes fell softly outside. Guests arrived in sleighs. I wore the ivory dress of my dreams, tiny pearl buttons trailing down the back. Candles glowed on the altar, and shiny ribbons pinned to the pews reflected their light. Pastor Brooks read us our vows, and we held hands and answered "I do" in quiet voices. Mary Anne and Suzanne stood with me, Henry and Joe Jr. with Frank.

My parents hosted a reception at their house. It seemed funny to think of it as *their* house instead of mine. But my home was with Frank now. He had inherited his parents' farm, and they moved up the hill to a smaller place.

When we arrived at the house, Frank helped me down from the wagon, and we greeted our guests as they arrived, horses trudging up the snowy mountain road. When all were inside, I turned to go in. Frank called out behind me. "Caroline!"

Before I could respond, a pack of wet snow smacked the back of my cape and an icy trickle ran down the back of my neck. I whirled around to see him grinning like a naughty schoolboy.

"You!" I reached down into the snow, packed it into a ball, cocked my right arm, and shot back. He ducked and ran to me, his large hands grabbing me around my waist. "Oh, how I love you, my dear Caroline," he said softly and planted a tender kiss on my lips.

Guests poured out of the house and into the fray, hurling snowballs at each other, red cheeked and shrieking.

That night, I quivered as we turned down the quilt and eased into bed. Frank took me in his strong arms.

"May we always have as much fun in our marriage as we are having tonight," he whispered.

Chapter Eighteen

October 1855

Frank was in the field baling the last of the hay when I felt the strongest kick. My baby was restless and soon would be ready to enter the world. When I told Frank months before that I was expecting, he scooped me into his arms and we danced in the front hallway, humming "The Bluebird Waltz," laughing.

The summer months seemed never ending, hot and humid. I felt as though I were carrying a watermelon in my womb as, out of breath and sweaty, I picked pole beans and swatted flies.

Moving out of my parents' house and into the Backus family home had been quite an adjustment for me. I was familiar with the place, having spent many hours there as a schoolgirl and for neighborhood gatherings. I knew well its feel and smell, the pine cabinets in the kitchen and the oak banister that lined the stairs. But it did not yet feel like "our" home. My mother-in-law was fond of wallpaper, and the dining room was lined with a light blue toile. The parlor furniture was heavier than I would have chosen, but I was grateful we had places to sit. I brought my quilts and writing desk and cooking pots to our new home, but it would take some time for this place to feel like our own.

My parents-in-law had moved to a smaller home just up the hill from us. It was a comfort to have them close by, but as the long hours passed as we waited for the baby, I grew lonely for my mother and tried to visit my parents as often as I could.

I felt a sudden, sharp pain as I stood in the kitchen that October afternoon. It was not a kick. It passed quickly, so I went on with my daily chores. I sat down at the table to peel vegetables. As I worked, a warmth spread beneath me. I stood up and saw a puddle on the chair and a wet spot on my skirt.

Jack, one of our farm hands, was chopping wood in the yard just outside the kitchen. I called to him through the open window and asked him to tell Frank to come quick. Another stabbing pain, and I sank back into the chair. I tried to slow my breathing, but it was a challenge.

After some time had passed, Frank rushed into the kitchen. "Is it time?" he asked, out of breath.

I nodded and winced as another pain pierced my womb. "Time to get your mother…Mama…"

Frank took my arm and helped me up the stairs to our bedroom. I leaned back into the pile of pillows and waited.

People came and went from the room as the labor pains grew sharper. My mother-in-law, Sally (I called her "Mother"), covered me with a crisp, clean sheet and set a pan of water on the bedside table. Mama arrived from Panther Mountain and put the kettle on. She sent for the midwife but was not sure if she would arrive in time as she was attending another birth in the county. Frank paced in and out of the room, taking my hand, wiping my brow. I prayed for a quick delivery but also knew from my sisters' birth stories that quick was asking quite a lot of God.

Someone opened a window as a strong contraction ripped through me. I arched my back and clutched at the mattress. I felt a cool cloth on my forehead and sank into the sheets as the pain passed and I braced for the next one. I could not tell how much time had passed. I tried to ask Mama, but my jaw was sore from clenching it tight and I was not making much sense.

I fixed my eyes on a crack in the ceiling. Mother reminded me to breathe steadily. I heard the word "chloroform," and I shook my head frantically as another pain pierced my abdomen. "No...no," I panted. I wanted to be awake for my baby's arrival, no matter how painful it was.

Some ladies from church were on their way with food for the family, a voice announced. It was my father-in-law calling up the stairs. As I floated in and out of a fog between contractions, I remembered overhearing some of those ladies at the baby shower fretting over the dangers of childbirth for "older" women. "The older they are, the harder their hip bones are," one said. "Oh dear," said the other. "I would not have thought of that." "Yes," said the first, "it is a medical fact. I thank our Lord Jesus that I began having mine at seventeen."

I tried so very hard not to cry out, but my pain would not be silent. No sign of Mrs. Brown, the midwife. The room was getting dark, which told me it had been at least six hours since labor began. Mama gave me a small sip of water, and it dribbled across my cheek.

In time, I heard "The midwife is here." It was Frank's voice. He knelt by my bedside. I gripped his arm so forcefully I thought I might break it in two, but I could not help myself. I felt someone lift the sheet up above my knees. "The head is crowning," Mrs. Brown announced in a firm and steady voice. "Keep pushing, Mrs. Backus. Keep breathing and pushing."

I strained as hard as I could, my neck a taut web of tendons and veins, sweat pouring into my eyes, hair stuck to my cheeks. "Push again, please. All right, you may rest for a moment."

I went limp and thought I could not possibly muster the strength to bear down one more time. "You can do it, Caroline," Mama whispered gently. "It won't be long now."

"Push again, please," Mrs. Brown ordered. I bore down as if birthing a pumpkin. Lord, I prayed, please help this baby out!

"Very good, Mrs. Backus. Here he comes!"

"A boy?" I cried out.

"Yes, and a healthy one at that. Look at the size of him!" Mother exclaimed. "Frank, come quick. Your son is here!"

I heard Frank bounding up the stairs. He stopped in the doorway, looking uncertain whether he should enter. My squirmy, wet son, red as a beet, lay on my stomach squalling as Mrs. Brown cut the cord.

"He's wonderful!" Frank exclaimed. He walked over to the bedside. "Caroline, what a fine son we have!"

I smiled weakly and sank back. The midwife cleaned the baby, wrapped him in a soft cotton blanket, and handed him to me as Frank puffed up the pillows behind my back so I could sit up a bit.

"Have you come up with a name?" Mama asked.

"Adam," Frank answered. "Because he is the first."

Chapter Nineteen

May 1861

The history of Virginia has been characterized by sectional antagonism. The natural features of her territory and the different elements in her population made such conflicts inevitable.

—*Sectionalism in Virginia from 1776 to 1861*, Charles Henry Ambler, Ph.D.

Adam enjoyed being the only child until he was three years old. He was surrounded by grandparents, aunts, uncles, and cousins who doted on him. It was a bit of a rude awakening for him when our second son, William Alexander, was born. And now I was pregnant again, expecting at the end of May.

What a frightening world we were bringing our new child into, though. Abraham Lincoln had been elected president in November and, one by one, Southern states broke off. South Carolina left first, in December. Three other states—Mississippi, Florida, and Alabama—followed in a matter of three days in January. Frank brought home copies of the *Virginia Weekly Star* from the post office, and we read reports of the proceedings at the state convention in Richmond. Although the delegates voted in February against recommending that Virginia secede from the Union, in March there were still rumblings in Western Virginia about dividing the state in two. Mr. Mortimer Dent wrote dispatches from the Richmond convention that month that reflected mountaineers' ongoing frustration with the Eastern Virginia planters. The state system was unfair. There was a limit to how much plantation owners could be taxed for their slaves, but no similar tax limit for other types of property.

"We, therefore, tell the people of Western Virginia," Dent wrote, "to prepare themselves for a separation from their Eastern brethren. It is bound to come sooner or later, and that being the case, the sooner the better. We call upon our people to stand up for their rights."

There was so much confusion and chaos that spring, as neighbors who had lived side by side in peace for so long were now divided and disputing with each other, some for the Union and some for the Southern cause. Our family knew where we stood: against slavery. I was filled with dread, however, that we might have to choose against our beloved Virginia.

It was a time of great lawlessness. Roving bands of ruffians swept through Western Virginia, stealing, burning, beating and threatening those who did not agree with their views, and sometimes taking those threats out on people and livestock. Some of these were just troublemakers spoiling for a fight, but many were secessionists— "secesh," we called them—who supported the new so-called republic, the Confederate States of America.

By April, our worst fears were realized. The Confederates attacked Fort Sumter, a federal fort in South Carolina, and war between the states officially began. A second vote on Virginia's secession was taken after the Fort Sumter attack. This time the outcome was different. Virginia tore away from the federal government and joined the CSA.

My state broke from the Union and swept us along with it. It felt as though we had been kidnapped. We did not know under what conditions we would live in what we considered to be a rogue nation.

112

What would life be like for our families, especially those of us who supported the Union? Would we have fair representation in the new government? Would we have the same court systems? What about those of us who were against secession and slavery? Would we be persecuted, arrested, tried for our beliefs?

Most Nicholas Countians did not waver in our support for the Union. Pressure was mounting around us because of our allegiance to the US government. Confederate friends were not so friendly, and many tried to recruit our men to fight for the CSA.

Why some Americans ever thought that trapping and enslaving Africans was a moral and Christian way to behave was beyond my thinking—I could not fathom it. But of course, I had gone over that argument with Nathan to no avail. I wondered if he was happy that Virginia was to be part of the new republic.

I was on high alert, ready to give birth at any moment while keeping a watchful eye out for strangers roaming our land. Frank kept a rifle over the mantel in the front room and had taught me how to use it should I need to. I was afraid to let Adam and Will play outside. My heart raced every time I heard the dogs bark.

We got word from upstate that the Union army attacked Confederate forces at Philippi. My uncle Sam Grose was an officer in a home guard formed to protect citizens in Nicholas and nearby counties, and he kept us abreast of the battles. Frank and his brothers joined the guard as well.

On May 28, our daughter Lucy was born, and we were somewhat removed from our worries for a while as we spent precious time with our newborn. William was not quite old enough to reckon who the new

113

baby was, but six-year-old Adam took his job as big brother very seriously and stood at the ready to fetch blankets and diapers as needed.

As spring spilled into summer, we were beset by unusually heavy rains. They were a blessing in that they probably deterred the bushwhackers from roaming our community. But the cooling showers could not quell the fiery hatred building between the North and South. Our beautiful mountains and valleys would soon be choked by a gunpowder haze and would soak up the blood of hundreds of men who were once fellow citizens of the great United States of America.

Chapter Twenty

Early August 1861

By late summer, the roads around the county were nothing but muck. A hot Virginia summer sun beat down on steamy clay. We were not going to town as frequently as usual because travel was treacherous, and not only because of the road conditions.

Bushwhackers—some pro-Confederate, others just thieves and jackals—were causing all sorts of trouble. Secesh sympathizers roamed in gangs and had stolen several horses from my sister Margaret's farm. We had no circuit rider at that time because it was simply too dangerous for them to ride through the woods. Guerilla fighters had taken to crouching behind thick mountain laurel and rhododendron bushes along county roads, waiting to ambush travelers. One family from our church, taking their wagon to town, were stopped at shotgun point on Summersville Road and robbed.

Around the first of the month, I left the children with Mother so that Frank and I could make a much-needed supply run. I scanned the thickets as Frank drove the horses down the mountain, wagon wheels creaking and sloshing through the muddy, rutted road. I was on alert, ready to grip the rifle stashed under my seat.

Frank tied up the horses in front of Hardman's. As I grabbed my basket out of the back of the wagon, I looked up Main Street and saw a group of about forty gray-uniformed men marching in order, clutching musket barrels tight to their shoulders, left arms swinging. Confederate troops had made their way to Summersville and were on parade to show all that they were there to secure the town.

"Traitors!" a man called from the sidewalk.

"Scalawag!" another man shot back. "Long live the South!"

The first man ran over to the second and swung at his chin. He missed, and the other man caught him in the left ear. The two struggled and fell into the muddy road near the troops, rolling and punching and kicking. Two of the soldiers left the formation, grabbed the fighters by their elbows, and pulled them away from each other.

"Halt!" The officer leading the band of soldiers turned to them and said, "Rest!"

They stepped back, right feet angled behind their left. The officer led them through a series of drills clearly designed to show the townspeople how well trained and prepared they were. I moved down the sidewalk in front of the store and saw that the officer was none other than Nathan.

"Would you look at that," Frank said in a low voice. "A Rebel lieutenant. Can't say I'm surprised."

I could not say a word. A sick feeling showered over me. I was angry, ashamed, disappointed, betrayed. I had tucked Nathan away into a corner of my memory, but seeing his sharp jaw and steely eyes brought up a sour taste in my mouth. I swallowed to hold back the bitter acid burning in my chest. Frank looked at me and said, "I think we've seen enough. Let's get what we need and get out of here."

The enemy had arrived. And I knew him well.

Chapter Twenty-One

August 1861

By Telegraph from Confederate General Henry A. Wise to General R. E. Lee, Commanding, from Bungers Mill, VA, Four Miles West of Lewisburg, Aug. 1st, 1861

The Kanawha Valley is wholly disaffected and traitorous. It was gone from Charleston down to Point Pleasant before I got there. Boone and Cabell are nearly as bad, and the state of things in Braxton, Nicholas and part of Greenbrier is awful. The militia are nothing for warlike uses here. They are worthless who are true, and there is no telling who is true. You cannot persuade these people that Virginia can or will ever reconquer the northwest, and they are submitting, subdued and debased.

By Telegraph from Gauley Bridge, Aug 4th 1861 via Galleopalis [sic], from Union Brigadier General J. D. Cox to Francis H. Pierpont, Governor of the "Loyal" or "Restored" Government of Virginia which was formed in Wheeling shortly after the state's Richmond government left the Union to join the Confederacy in May 1861.

I have about eight hundred [800] serviceable muskets with bayonets taken from the enemy they are at your disposal for the purpose you mentioned. I would suggest the sending of some reliable Officer as agent to the Valley to act for you in the formation of companies of Union Home guards issuing commissions and arms & numbers are anxious to join in Fayette issuing the muskets.

Soldiers from both sides of the conflict flooded into Nicholas County that month. Union troops were stationed at Gauley Bridge, a few miles from Panther Mountain, and Confederates held the rocky cliffs around Hawk's Nest. It was only a matter of time before shots were fired.

August 24, 1861

The 7th Ohio Volunteer Infantry arrived at the foot of our mountain a little more than a week after we saw the Rebels in town. Frank saw the troops staking tarps and moving canteen supplies into a base camp on his ride home from guard duty. As soon as he told us about their encampment, I went to the kitchen to cook up some food for the troops. My sisters came over to help. Jerusha peeled and sliced apples while Mary Anne worked flour, shortening, and salt into pie crusts and hardtack. I sliced ham and cheese and ladled pinto beans into jars.

My sisters and I rode our horses down to the foot of the mountain where we saw dozens of tents dotting the field. I was overwhelmed by the smell of damp iron and horse manure, and nervous about approaching the troops. The flies were thick, and the soldiers' boots made sucking sounds as the men walked through their muddy camp.

Seeing the soldiers filled me with both relief and dread, as I realized that, while they had come to protect our homes against the Rebel troops, the war had officially reached our doorstep. They all looked so young, baby faced even. As we ladled out beans and passed out slices of

118

pie, we learned that many of them had been students in Ohio but left their studies to fight for the Union.

"Thank you kindly, ma'am," said one to me as I handed him a packet of hardtack. "We are mighty tired and hungry, having marched back and forth in terrible conditions in the past few days. My name is Martin," he said as he tipped his cap at me, revealing a thick head of wavy brown hair. "Martin Andrews." His eyes were the color of milkweed, his young, fresh cheeks dotted with stubble.

"You are very welcome, Martin. We are grateful that you all have come here to defend our Union. Where are you from?"

"I come from Cleveland, Ohio, ma'am. I was a student at Oberlin College when the war broke out. A great number of my classmates and I enlisted right after the attack on Sumter."

"You made a difficult decision, then, to leave your education to fight for our country," I said. "Surely you must miss the student's life?"

"What I miss most are books, ma'am. But there isn't much reading time for a soldier."

"Which books are among your favorites?" I asked.

"I enjoy the classics but also some contemporary authors. Hugo. Poe. Longfellow's poetry is exquisite."

"You are mentioning writers I greatly admire as well," I said.

"Well then, I am in good company," he said with a smile. "I must go now, but thank you again." I watched him walk over to a lean-to and stuff the food packet into his haversack.

I rode on horseback down the mountain the next morning. I was hoping I'd see Martin. I had brought him a book to take with him. But the soldiers of Company C were gone. The company's cook was packing pots and pans into the back of a wagon. He told us he would be joining the soldiers at Kessler's Cross Lanes. I slipped *Moby-Dick* back into my saddlebag, sorry that I had not been able to give it to Martin before he left. As I rode back up the mountain, I thought about how anxious his parents must have been when he told them he would leave the relative safety of a college campus and head into war.

Frank was waiting for me on the front porch as I trotted Pansy up the lane. He seemed agitated and was pacing back and forth. He was wearing his cloth hunting coat and had a blue kerchief tied around his neck.

"I wish you wouldn't go out alone. It's too dangerous. I worry when you're gone so long," he called out. "I'm going with the home guard tonight. We hear there might be a fight at Cross Lanes. We need to be on the lookout for..."

"It wears on my nerves that you might get hurt out there on patrol," I called back as I dismounted and tied my horse to the post. My throat tightened as I walked up to him on the porch.

"I know," he said, eyes softening. He reached over and squeezed my arm. "You and the children should go over to your parents'. Let's pick up Mother and Father on the way. They can stay with Henry and Mary Anne."

I hurried into the house and dashed from room to room, wiping my clammy palms on a folded diaper and stuffing our clothes and supplies into a bag. My head was buzzing as I strained to remember every item

120

we might need. My temples pounding, I watched Frank through the bedroom window as he loaded sacks, saddle bags, and muskets into the back of the wagon. He was heading straight into danger. What if pickets attacked him on the road? What if he was caught in the crossfire of the battle?

Later, we heard gunfire crackling down in the valley as we pulled up to the front of my parents' house just as the sun was setting.

Frank hopped down and came around to help me down from the wagon. He put his hands on my waist and gently helped me to the ground. He paused for a moment, his eyes searching mine, and put a hot hand to my cheek. I clasped his hand with trembling fingers.

"Be careful, my love," I whispered.

***

The shots died down as darkness fell over the farm. Still, I had a restless night in my old bedroom, which was stuffy and hot. Will and Adam slept sweaty but soundly on two cots next to my bed, Lucy in the old family crib at the foot. I worried about Frank and the rest of the men in his guard group, whether they had the numbers and arms to fend off attackers and defend the mountain. My mind was busy making plans. If intruders came to the house, Mama and I would take the children to the center hall closet and hide. Or if we were outside, we would go into the root cellar.

Dawn was just breaking when musket fire filled the air, faster and more intense than the night before. This time the sound was accompanied by cannon fire rumbling through the valley and vibrating our wood floor.

121

The noise woke Lucy, and she cried to be picked up from her crib. As I lifted her out, Adam sat up from his cot and rubbed his eyes.

"What's all that racket, Mama?" he asked in a crackly voice. Will squinted one sleepy eye at me.

"Our Union men are defending us at Cross Lanes, dear. We shall pray for them, and I'm sure they will win," I said, fighting to keep my voice soft and steady so that the boys would not sense my fear that our side would not prevail.

Mama and I busied ourselves making breakfast after we all lumbered down the stairs. The smell of spent gunpowder hung heavy in the damp air. Dishes on shelves rattled ever so slightly each time a boom came up from the land below.

Frank arrived in the afternoon, exhausted. He was off duty for a few hours and needed food and rest before going back. A Yankee scout had told him the Rebels attacked at Cross Lanes, just four miles away.

"We heard they surprised the Yanks this morning while they were eating their breakfast," he said.

He excused himself and went to lie down. The heat was stifling; the children were red cheeked and sweaty. I laid Will in a crib in the back bedroom, which was cooler thanks to the shade of a mighty oak on that side of the house. Adam and I went out to the back porch for some fresh air. We listened to the racket echoing off the mountains. He asked me if a thunderstorm was coming.

It was no easy task to explain war to a six-year-old. I told him that his papa was helping protect our land and that there were some people

122

who were trying to rebel against our government and President Lincoln. I told him the troublemakers would not win and that slaves would someday be free. I hoped I was right.

Chapter Twenty-Two

August 1861

Get ready; be prepared, you and all the hordes gathered about you, and take command of them. After many days you will be called to arms. In future years you will invade a land that has recovered from war, whose people were gathered from many nations to the mountains of Israel, which had long been desolate. They had been brought out from the nations, and now all of them live in safety. You and all your troops and the many nations with you will go up, advancing like a storm; you will be like a cloud covering the land.

—Ezekiel 38:7–9

Frank stuffed his satchel with a packet of cornbread and bacon and left on horseback in early evening to rejoin the guard. After supper, I put the children to bed and came back downstairs to join my parents in the parlor.

"Where will this madness lead?" Mama wondered out loud.

"The Rebs will not give up without a big fight, I know that," Papa said. "I pray our Yanks will hold firm."

I stared at the guns over the fireplace and looked back down at my needlework. "I pray the president will stand firm as well. He must mend our country."

The fire burned low. Papa held out a hand to Mama on the couch. "Listen." He paused and turned his head. "The shots are coming fewer and farther between. Are you going up soon, Caroline?"

"I'll stay here awhile. I'll make sure the fire's out. Good night."

My needle poked strands of red yarn down and up through the cloth, working on a needlepoint American flag that would hang in our living room when it was finished.

I must have nodded off on the couch. Just a few red coals were glowing in the fireplace when I was startled awake by the sound of footsteps on the back porch. Fear shot through me. I dropped my work and grabbed the lantern next to me, carried it to the fireplace and plucked down Papa's favorite rifle, checking to make sure it was loaded. I stalked toward the parlor door and peered into the kitchen. A shadow ducked back and forth at the kitchen door, lit from the back by the bright moonlight. The doorknob clanked as it twisted back and forth.

I pulled the gun butt tight into the crook of my right shoulder, my cheek pressing the stock hard, the way Frank had shown me, and froze for a moment. Could it be Frank? No, I could make out a soldier's cap on the shadowy figure. Then another body loomed behind the one at the door.

There was banging, loud and heavy. "Who's there?" I yelled, squinting through the sight, my finger on the trigger.

"Seventh Ohio Volunteer Infantry, ma'am!" a young voice shouted. "Can you help us, please?"

Papa scrambled down the steps. "What is it? Who goes there?"

"Union army, sir!" the voice shouted again. I lowered the rifle, and Papa unlatched and opened the back door. There stood a gaggle of blue-uniformed soldiers, lit from behind by the low-hanging moon. "Permission to come inside, sir," an officer barked.

"Yes, of course," said my father, extending his arm toward the kitchen table. "Come in."

Mama came into the kitchen in her nightcap, tying her robe around her. "How many of you are there?" she exclaimed as muddy soldiers piled in, smelling of sweat and gunpowder.

"More than a dozen, ma'am," the officer answered. "Sorry for the intrusion. We had no choice but to run for the hills after the battle."

"How did you make out?" Papa asked him.

"Not well, sir. Several in our company were wounded and left behind. The rest of us headed for the hills."

"Land sakes," Mama said, shaking her head. "Well, get yourselves in here and wash up. We'll treat those who need it."

I went to the cupboard and grabbed antiseptic, salve, and cotton off the shelf. The officer was looking over his troops, checking for wounds and powder burns.

I picked away at a block in the icebox and wrapped ice chips in strips of cloth. Papa and some of the soldiers headed to the well with lanterns and buckets. All the commotion woke Adam, and he stood, wide-eyed, at the kitchen door in his nightshirtpajamas.

"Darling, you must go back to bed," I cautioned. "We are helping our soldiers after their battle. Go on back upstairs."

"Mama, no, please. I want to help!" Adam cried. I smiled at my son. I knew he was fascinated by soldiers and their weapons. This was a show he could not miss.

"All right then, but stand off in the corner near the pantry."

Papa and the troops returned with buckets sloshing, and we set up a wash stand on the kitchen table for the men. Mama and I tended to cuts and burns. No one in the group appeared to be seriously injured, no bullet wounds, just some gashed arms and legs and sprained ankles.

Adam fetched clean sheets from the linen closet, and I instructed him to lay them across the parlor floor so that the soldiers could sit down and remove their packs without spreading too much filth on the braided rugs. Papa gathered up canteens and filled them with fresh water. He invited all to rest on the parlor floor before we served them a bite to eat.

After my light medical duty, I lit the stove and pulled out a canister of flour for biscuit making. I turned to fetch the rolling pin and noticed that the young soldier washing up at the table looked familiar. It was Martin from Oberlin, whom I had met at the temporary camp.

"Well, you are a sight for sore eyes!" I exclaimed. "Martin, isn't it?"

"Yes, ma'am," he said, wiping his face with a towel. "How nice to see you again."

"I am glad you made it safely through the battle. Where does your company go from here?"

127

"We are to regroup at Gauley Bridge as soon as possible," he answered.

"I wish we could do more for you than just feed you," I said. And then I remembered how I'd brought him a book after the soldiers had broken camp. I went to the parlor and pulled down *Moby-Dick*.

I walked back into the kitchen. "At least I can give you something to take with you that might take your mind off this horrible war, if only for a few moments," I said as I handed him the book.

He grinned at me. "What a wonderful gift. Thank you so much."

I excused myself and took Adam to bed. On the way up the stairs, he said, "Mama, can I join the Union army? I want to help them fight the Rebs."

I grabbed his hand. "No, my sweetheart, you are too young, and besides, my heart would break from missing you if you were to be away at war. The best way you can help our Yanks is to pray for them each and every night before you go to bed."

"I promise I will," he said as we reached the bedroom door. "Good night, Mama."

Chapter Twenty-Three

September 10, 1861

We moved slowly and cautiously through the days after the Battle of Cross Lanes. Sun-dried clay was firmer underfoot than in muddy weeks past, and an early autumn haze hung over the mountain. The gunfire had ended, but we knew that rangers sympathetic to the South were lurking in the brush. Colonel Floyd's soldiers set up pickets on my sister Margaret's farm and pressed her husband, James, so hard to join the Confederate cause that he slipped away in the dark of night to Ohio. He planned to move their family there so that they could escape the dangers of Western Virginia. Margaret insisted on staying home on Panther Mountain with their seven children. I considered her very brave for staying put without James there to help protect them.

I picked at my eggs and ham with a fork, and the children quietly munched cornbread around the kitchen table on the morning of September 10. The rumble of galloping hoofs headed toward our house shook us from our meal.

"Firefight at Carnifex Ferry!" Uncle Sam Grose shouted from outside. "All men to your posts!"

Frank went to the front door. "Where?" he yelled.

"Henry Patterson's farm. We got 'em outnumbered."

Not again, I thought. Would this be our life from now on? Another battle in little more than a week. Adam ran into the room.

"Who's fighting?" he shouted, his cheeks pink with excitement.

"Simmer down, son." Frank waved at him as he strained to hear Sam barking out orders for the militia. He stepped out on the porch as our farmhand Jacob burst out of our shed.

I smoothed my son's unruly blond hair and told him as much as I dared of what we'd heard from Sam. "Our Union soldiers found a nest of Rebels nearby. Let's pray for their safety." We held hands and asked God to protect all of the soldiers battling at the ferry.

"Why should we pray for the Rebs?" Adam asked when we had finished, his blue eyes holding me in a stern gaze.

"Well, Jesus taught us to pray for everyone, even our enemies. This terrible war has stirred up hatred between North and South, but we must remember that we are all God's children, every one of us, no matter which side of the war we're on." He shook his head and pressed his lips together.

We now had a Restored Government of Virginia in Wheeling with a governor whom President Lincoln officially recognized. Frank and I and our families all supported the idea of Western Virginia becoming a new and separate state. Methodist Episcopal pastors strongly urged our congregation to vote in favor of statehood; many clergymen were involved in pro-Union causes and were running for public office.

Bushwhacking and general lawlessness continued, so much so that President Lincoln had declared Nicholas and surrounding counties to be under martial law. We had no official law enforcement—no sheriff or police—and no courts in session. The courthouse was shuttered; no one was recording births, deaths, or marriages.

I walked out onto the porch. "Would you please go with the children?" Frank asked me as he loaded his rifle. Cannon fire boomed down in the valley.

"No, there is too much to do here on the farm. With you out on patrol, I need to work in the fields. I will be fine. Don't worry."

It was up to me to harvest the last of the sweet corn before it dried up. We wouldn't have enough to last us through winter if I didn't. Jacob was on guard duty and couldn't come help me.

Frank looked at me for a long time and then took my hand. "I don't know what I would do without you." His eyes were puffy and bloodshot. The war was taking its toll on him.

"You won't have to find out," I said, kissing his hand and giving him my best brave smile. "I'll get the children ready."

Frank took Lucy, Will, and Adam to his parents' house up the road on his way to his guard post. Apron and boots on, Frank's revolver in my right hand, scythe in my left, I sang as I walked to the cornfield.

"Bringing in the sheaves, bringing in the sheaves,

We shall come rejoicing, bringing in the sheaves."

God blessed us with a good harvest that year. Yet I wondered why He had allowed the war to tear through our lives. Danger was all around us, but still we had to try to live our lives as normally as possible, knowing that our crops, our livestock, our home could be gone in an instant.

The scythe blade sliced through the stalks, and they fell in clumps to the ground. All at once, I heard voices. I stood up straight and wiped my brow. Through the woods, a small cluster of gray-clad men clambered over tree stumps about a hundred yards away from where I was working. Rebs. My spine turned to ice.

The soldiers came towards me, their grimy, sunburned faces laughing, mocking. Three of them. They stank. I held the scythe tightly.

"Well look there, the little lady farmer," one sneered. "Why ain't your husband out here in the fields helpin' you?"

"Ain't this the mountain where the stinkin' Yankees run cryin' after we whip 'em?" said another.

"Is you or is you ain't a bluebelly?"

"I beg your pardon?" My voice was breathy as I took a step back.

"You a Yankee lover, lady?"

"You have no right to trespass on our land," I shot back. I knew I could not outrun them but continued to step back, toward the spot on the ground where the gun lay. "You'd best be on your way."

"Aw no, we cain't do that, lady. We poor starvin' soldiers need a bite to eat. Maybe you could cook us some o' this here corn?"

They gathered closer around me. I raised the curved blade in my hand and sliced at them. "I'm warning you! Git!"

One laughed at me, revealing his rotten teeth. "You cain't talk to us that way! We will soon own this here mountain! You'll soon be eatin' with the pigs!"

They jumped back as I threw the scythe at the three of them. The blade nicked one soldier on the leg, tearing his pants; he cried out and fell to the ground. I reached down into a pile of sheaves, pulled out the revolver, steadied it with my left hand and squeezed off a shot into the air above their heads.

"Think I won't do it?" I yelled at them. Five shots, I thought, just five more shots. I cocked the hammer again as one doubled back and fell into the cornstalks. The fall knocked his weapon out of his hand. Another pulled his gun, and I aimed at his head. "Don't try it!"

They backed down the path to the woods, and one took off running, the others following. Cowards. I shot at the trees around them, and one tripped and fell, then scrambled off after the others.

I ran to the house and bolted the lock, still grasping the revolver. I waited by the window in case they came back.

***

The sun was setting when I heard the horses' clop-clopping as Frank and the children rolled up in the wagon. I was half-asleep in a chair, hand still grasping the gun butt.

"Mama!" Adam cried out after he burst through the door. "Why are you holding that gun?"

I adjusted my eyes to see him. I saw before me in the living room not my son but a little girl wearing a robin's egg blue calico dress and bonnet. "Son?" I murmured as I sat upright.

"Look at how Grandma Backus dressed me up. Isn't it a funny sight?"

My boy was indeed wearing a dress and looked for all the world like a six-year-old girl. "Why are you dressed like that?"

Frank walked into the room carrying Lucy. "Rebs were at Mother and Father's, trying to take Adam."

"What?"

"They are swarming the mountain, setting up on farms, trying to recruit even young boys as drummers for their companies. Mother found one of Sister's old dresses and put it on him so they would think he was a girl and leave him alone."

"Oh my Lord," I said with a catch in my throat. "What evil to force children into battle! Oh...."

Frank put Lucy down on the floor and came over to my chair. He gently took the gun from my hand and knelt down, putting his arm around me. "I am fine, Mama," Adam said as he walked toward me, tripping a bit on his skirt. "I was quiet when they came to the house, but I wanted to yell awful things at them!"

"You did the right thing, son," Frank said to him. "Why don't you go take off that silly dress?"

Adam nodded and left the room.

"Why *are* you holding my revolver?"

Looking into my husband's tired eyes made me want to crumble. I cleared my throat.

"Stinkin' Rebs came to the cornfield while I was working. They surrounded me, but I fought them off with the scythe and got to the gun before they could do me any harm."

Frank's face reddened. "I asked you to go to my parents' house, but you were too stubborn!"

"We have got to get these crops in before the frost!" I shot back. "What with you and Jacob on guard, how else will we get that done? We could starve this winter if we don't bring in the corn."

"Nothing is more important than your safety!"

I swallowed hard. "Well, I think I did a fairly good job of keeping myself safe, don't you? And even if I had gone to Mother and Father's, the Rebs showed up there, too!" My face was hot.

Frank paced on the rug. "I am just sick that you could have been hurt...or worse."

"I am sick of this war." I sank back into the chair. Lucy's wispy blond strands glowed in the firelight as she sat near the hearth. Tears ran down her little cheeks.

My husband walked over to me and held out his hands. I stood and wrapped my arms around his waist. He squeezed me, put a hand on my cheek, and kissed me. "I am sick of it, too. I pray it will soon be over. But until that time, we must be brave."

I am sad to say that the war was not soon over, not at all.

Chapter Twenty-Four

September 11, 1861

Carnifex Ferry, Virginia

As I drove the horses up the road to Henry Patterson's farm, I saw a bloody mess. Men's bodies were strewn like broken toys tossed across mud and grass. Ragged, crimson-soaked cloth hung from arms and legs that were twisted and bent in ways God never meant them to be. Black smoke rose up the cliff from where fragments of ferry boats, charred after the Confederate retreat, littered the rushing waters of the Gauley River below.

Suzanne, Mary Anne, and Margaret were with me. We brought a load of clean flour sacks ready to rip into bandage strips, along with ointments, food, and water.

I tied the horses at the Pattersons' hitching post. Margaret handed me boxes and bottles from the wagon. The stench of decaying flesh mixed with metal and manure hung in the humid air. I brought my handkerchief up to my nose. My eyes watered.

Frank, Henry, and dozens of other local men dug up hunks of dirt with spades and shovels, creating a makeshift graveyard in the barnyard. The outer log walls of the farmhouse were pocked and splintered, the work of hundreds of bullets.

Under a white tent near the Pattersons' house, rows of soldiers lay covered in white sheets on cots. Mary Anne and Margaret took baskets of biscuits and custard around to those wounded who were able to sit up and eat. I walked over and laid a box of our home medicines on the ground next to the cot of a soldier, eyes closed, a bloody hand draped across his stomach.

"Sir, may I give you some water?" I asked as I crouched down next to him. He squinted at me and nodded. I was afraid to touch him, but knew he needed help. I slid my left hand beneath his pillow and propped his head up, then brought a canteen up to his lips.

The soldier's face was shiny and grimy with gunpowder. He choked a bit, so I lifted his head slightly, my heart beating hard. "Were you shot in the hand?"

He nodded again. "That's the only wound, I think," he answered. "I am just so weary...." He reared his head back and wilted back down on the bed.

"We are not nurses, but we are here to help in any way we can," Suzanne said softly as she came up beside me with a bowl of warm water and a clean rag. He winced as she gingerly dabbed around the caked blood on his palm.

It seemed to me that the best way to distract him while she dressed his wound was to ask him a bit about himself.

"Do I hear a bit of an Irish accent, sir?"

"Aye," he answered, looking up at me. His eyes were light blue, his nose ever so slightly upturned. "I have come from Ohio, but before that, County Mayo."

Suzanne asked him his name. "Patrick," he said. "Patrick Gilligan."

"Well, Patrick Gilligan, thank you for fighting here for our Union," she said, her hand lightly touching his bandaged hand. "We are most grateful."

He pressed his lips together. "It is a noble cause, worth fighting for, ma'am. We lost some good men here yesterday, including Colonel Lowe, a fine leader. But we have won the Kanawha Valley and sent the Rebs packin' across the river."

"Indeed you have," I said, smiling. "And we are very grateful for that."

Suzanne and I left Patrick to rest. As we washed up at a tin basin, we heard a sudden, sharp shriek from the next tent over; no doubt a reaction to a surgeon's scalpel digging bullets from a soldier's skin.

"All of this blood." Suzanne shook her head. "All of this pain. Is it worth the sacrifice?"

For once, I didn't have an answer for her.

Chapter Twenty-Five

July 25, 1862

For the last eight or ten days, we have been quartered at Summerville [sic], the county site of Nicholas County. This was once, no doubt, a nice and flourishing little village, and the country around indicates that peace, happiness and plenty once resided here; but, with the approach of the invading foe, these things have all passed away, And in their stead, there is now little else seen than distress, want and ruin. The village, and all the country around, wear the aspect of some disconsolate widow draped in robes of sable hue, mourning a brighter and a better day.

—Letter from Confederate soldier to editor of *The Abingdon Virginian*, 1862

Clouds of black smoke curled up through the air above town. The stench of burned wood and animal flesh wafted on the breeze. Summersville was burning.

Union troops, stationed in town, were under attack. We stood on a cliff at the edge of Henry and Mary Anne's farm on Panther Mountain and watched the distant destruction.

"I thought the Ninth West Virginia could fend 'em off," Henry said, shaking his head. "Guess I was wrong."

"What will we do?" Mary Anne cried, her forehead creased. "Hardman's is almost gone. Where will we shop? We are losing everything!"

Henry slid his arm across her shoulders. No one answered her. Our town was on fire, and at that moment, it seemed as though our whole world had fallen through to Hades.

My fifteen-year-old nephew, Will Renick, rode up the mountain on a shiny black horse to where we stood on the cliff. "The Moccasin Rangers and Confederate cavalry attacked the Ninth. I saw 'em ride in. They took some officers prisoner, raided the supplies and ammunition. Then they set fire to the Valley House hotel, the Catholic church, the telegraph office, and some houses along Main Street."

Will's face was smudged with soot, and he was breathing hard. "Come inside and let's get you washed up and rested," I said as I took his elbow and guided him toward the front porch.

We later read in the *Point Pleasant Register* that the Moccasin Rangers or "Mocs," a local guerilla group, had indeed alerted the Rebs and led the charge into Summersville. There were more than two hundred of them. Some from the Ninth West Virginia were able to escape. Their secesh cousins recognized them and gave them a head start before they began firing.

Pastor Ian Murphy shared that information when we met at the Hinkles' home a week after the attack. My niece Lydia offered to watch the children so that Frank and I could both attend the meeting. The Hinkle farm was below ours on the mountain. Martha and Joe Hinkle had a beautiful clapboard home shaded in thick forest, surrounded by laurel and rhododendron. A number of our Panther Mountain neighbors sat in their parlor that hot July evening, sweating and fanning ourselves with pamphlets that spelled out the statehood bill that had passed in the U.S. Senate just a week before.

About a dozen of us gathered there, anxious to hear more about the proposed new state. Frank and I sat next to Elijah and Polly Walker on a bench. Even Harman Dawes, the former town drunk, joined us. Harman had finally found Jesus and sworn off of alcohol. His gray hair was combed back, and although he was up in years, he sat straight and tall on a ladder-back chair in his brown suit coat.

"Thank you all for coming," said Pastor Murphy, addressing us as he stood in front of the Hinkles' living room fireplace. He was a native-born Irishman, tall and thick. His red hair—what was left of it—clumped around his ears and the back of his head. His Irish brogue flavored his words.

"Your support is so very critical for the future of our new West Virginia. Shall we pray?"

A stately grandfather clock ticked as we bowed our heads.

"Almighty God, we come before you today in this house to ask for your divine wisdom and discernment. You know how dearly we cherish our church, our community, our freedom, and how deeply in danger we are in the midst of this horrible war. Please send your angels to stand, shining heavenly swords blazing, between us and the enemy. And please guide President Lincoln, our members of Congress, our state convention leaders, and especially our Methodist Episcopal delegates to act on behalf of all people of West Virginia. Surely, Lord, we face uncertainty at this difficult time, but we thank you for your never-ending love and peace that passes all understanding. For all these things we pray. Amen."

Pastor Murphy's eyes lit up as he paced back and forth in front of the crowd. It felt like a camp meeting right there in the room. "Friends, you have a choice to make. Your choice is to decide whether you will urge members of the Congress to make our beautiful West Virginia the first state born of civil war. Our other option is not desirable—no, not at all. If we remain under Richmond rule, dear friends, we will face persecution or worse! You may believe we are persecuted now. If we do not vote to break away, we may be broken!"

Pastor Murphy explained to us that the statehood bill had several more hurdles to cross. The House of Representatives would have to pass it, President Lincoln would have to approve the creation of West Virginia as a state loyal to the Union without abolishing slavery, sign it into law and then, after all that, we citizens would have to vote in favor of West Virginia's creation as the thirty-fifth state.

Elijah, whom I knew from church, raised his hand. "Pastor, I am sorely disappointed that our U.S. senators passed a bill that does not offer freedom for slaves as soon as statehood is granted." Heads nodded and tongues clucked in agreement.

"Well, Elijah, I share your disappointment. I and a majority of my fellow pastors were in favor of West Virginia entering the Union as a free state. It appears that our elected representatives did not believe such a bill would pass the Senate. However, the Willey Amendment to the bill does call for gradual abolition."

I shivered a bit as I thought back to the time when Andy and I discovered the shackle in the cave. How we and the Backuses and Pastor Sam spirited Edward into our barn in the dark of night. How my heart pounded as I watched Papa drive the wagon away the next morning, past the patrollers, with Edward tucked into one of the barrels. No more slavery. That had been our dream for so long, it was hard to believe that it could even come true.

The meeting broke up just as the sun was easing its way down through purple and pink streaks in the sky. Even a lovely sunset could not settle my mind as I wondered whether we could possibly become West Virginians or not.

"I am hopeful and yet worried at the same time," Frank said to me as we walked over to our wagon. "So much depends on so many different people making the right decision."

I nodded, and then someone cried out, "Stop right there! Stop or we'll shoot!" A crack of gunfire shattered the evening air.

Frank pushed me against the side of the wagon and stood in front of me. I grabbed his elbow, hands shaking, and pressed into his back to steady myself.

"Get over there!" a man on horseback shouted, jerking his rifle toward the Hinkles' barn. Everyone leaving the Hinkle house, including Pastor Murphy, was surrounded by about twenty bushwhackers wearing a motley variety of gray caps, bandanas around their necks, rifles cocked.

As Polly Walker jerked her hands up, she dropped onto the grass a copy of the *Pittsburgh Christian Advocate*, the pro-Union, pro-statehood newspaper that often gave us news of where Confederate guerillas were hiding out. We held our hands above our heads, tripping over rocks and roots as we headed to the barn.

"Traitors!" one of the men shouted. "What do you have to say for yourselves?" He walked over to the newspaper on the ground, picked it up and wagged it at us. "This rag isn't worthy of wiping a Confederate ass!"

"Y'all can get arrested in parts of Virginia just for reading this!" a black-haired bushwhacker wearing a red bandana yelled at us.

"We are Union here!" someone cried out. It was Harman Dawes.

"Shut up, old man!" the man with the bandana yelled. "We are Thurmond's Rangers, here to hold this part of Virginia for the Confederate States of America!" He pointed his gun at Harman.

"I will not shut up! God bless the United States of America! God bless the Union!"

The Ranger who appeared to be the group's captain shouted, "McClung! Hold your fire!"

But McClung pulled the trigger and a single shot rang out, causing me to flinch. At the same moment, Harman cried out in pain and fell to the ground, clutching his bloodied thigh.

I ran over to him and pulled off my scarf, wrapping it around his upper leg to slow the bleeding. "Caroline!" Frank called after me. "No!"

As I crouched down to help Harman, I felt something hard pressed up against the back of my head. I heard Martha Hinkle gasp and realized that it was a gun. "Stand up, Yankee scum!" McClung spat out.

I rose slowly, hands up, and was guided at gunpoint to the side of the barn. "All of you! Stand next to her!"

Two of the Rangers were holding Frank from behind by the arms. He struggled to get free but couldn't break the men's grip. They shoved him into the rough, red wood of the barn, where we all were lined up. I could not stop shivering. The air cooled as the last evening light faded and the bright moon rose. *We will be executed this night,* I thought. Tears ran down my cheeks as I thought of Adam, Will, and Lucy. *Lord, please don't let us die!* I screamed inside my head.

Someone lit a pine torch, then another. Flickering flames shone on our fearful faces. "Please don't shoot us! Have mercy on us!" a woman said, sobbing.

Then, the sound of horse hoofs thundered up a back road behind the Hinkles' farm. *More Rangers?* I thought. The pounding grew louder. I saw gray-uniformed men riding toward us, torches in their hands.

A clutch of about eight Confederate soldiers rode up to us. I could make out stripes on one officer's sleeve. His eyes glowed in the torchlight. Familiar eyes. I knew them.

"What goes on here?" a deep voice boomed. It was Nathan. Lieutenant Nathan Hanna. "Cap'n Thurmond?"

"Yes, sir, we caught these folks leaving a meeting," Thurmond answered. "They were plotting against the state of Virginia and have illegal papers in their possession."

The lieutenant was quite a picture, mounted on his horse, in his crisp uniform. His cap covered all but a few tufts of curly silver hair.

Nathan scanned our faces lined up against the barn wall and stopped at mine. In the torchlight, I could see his sharp stare soften.

He turned back to Thurmond. "Why is this man hurt?"

145

"One of my men tried to shut him up and took things too far," Thurmond said through gritted teeth, glaring at McClung.

Nathan motioned to one of his soldiers to go over and help Harman. "All right then," he said to the guerillas, "we will take care of these traitors. You are relieved of your duty."

Captain Thurmond gave him a wary look. "Yes, sir," he said with a choppy salute. "Stand down, men!" The ragtag bunch looked at each other, frozen for a moment, not knowing whether to move. "You are dismissed!" Thurmond barked at them. One by one, they mounted their horses and slowly trotted down the mountain road.

"Private, help the man onto your horse," Nathan ordered one of his men. "We will take him to the medicine tent on the way to the jail."

Nathan turned to address us. "As for you, I should take you all as my prisoners for your treasonous act. I warn you, do not gather together again like this or you will be arrested and tried in military court. Go back to your families. Take the back road." His eyes met mine once more. Then he turned to his soldiers, nodded, and led them down the mountain on the front road.

I ran into Frank's arms, and he hugged me tight. I pressed my head to his chest and felt his heart pounding hard.

"I cannot believe he let us go," I said, my voice quivering.

"I can," Frank said. "I think you saved all of us."

Chapter Twenty-Six

June 1863

The division of a State is dreaded as a precedent. But a measure made expedient by a war, is no precedent for times of peace. It is said the admission of West Virginia is secession, and tolerated only because it is our secession. Well, if we can call it by that name, there is still difference enough between secession against the Constitution, and secession in favor of the Constitution.

–President Abraham Lincoln

Our state this day is free in fact... Not made free by the bayonet, but by the living principles of immutable truth, which we as a church maintain.

—A West Virginia Methodist

An early summer rain washed the dusty streets of Summersville clean just in time. The still-charred stone walls of the telegraph office and freshly repaired and painted porch of the Valley House hotel stood as reminders of the violence our community had endured to break from the eastern counties and join the Union.

Crowds of people from all around the county came to celebrate our victory. Mountain voters spoke loud and clear at the ballot box, and the new state of West Virginia was born, baptized by President Lincoln and the U.S. Congress.

Our family stood on the courthouse lawn and watched hundreds of people gather in the streets and on sidewalks: ladies in bounteous hoop skirts, men in top hats, boys in knee pants, and girls in calico dresses, hair tied with ribbons. The sharp lines of soldiers' uniforms, mostly blue, cut fine figures around the perimeter of the crowd. Red, white, and blue flags and buntings were everywhere—waving in hands, adorning brick buildings and buggies. A brass band provided music from the town square gazebo.

Pat McCutcheon burst out of the telegraph office on Main Street waving a telegram high in the air. He ran to the courthouse steps, pushed his wire glasses up on his nose, adjusted his visor, and cleared his throat.

"Ladies and gentlemen, here is the news from Wheeling," he announced and began to read the telegram.

"'Wheeling, West Virginia. June twentieth, 1863.

"'This day ushers into being the new State of West Virginia and adds the thirty-fifth star to the constellation of the American Union. STOP.

"'The old Government goes out and the new one comes in. STOP. Today Governor Pierpont bids us a formal farewell and Gov. Boreman will be inaugurated as his successor. STOP. Today the Legislature of the new State meets for organization.'"

The crowd burst into shouts. "Hurrah!" "Long live West Virginia!" "God bless the United States of America!" "God bless President Lincoln!" Hats of all types flew into the air above Main Street.

Then other shouts came.

"Boo!" "We will not give up the fight!" "Down with West Virginia!" "God bless President Jefferson Davis!"

A group of men wearing work shirts and dungarees broke into song:

"Our Dixie forever!

She's never at a loss!

Down with the eagle

And up with the cross!"

The chorus was drowned out by booing and shushing onlookers. Mayor John Jones and Pastor Murphy joined Pat on the courthouse steps as a majority of people applauded.

I picked Lucy up and cradled her in my arms. My heart swelled as I looked around. We had snatched our mountain home back from secession. I only wished that I could have cast a ballot for statehood. I looked at my beautiful light-haired daughter, kissed her soft cheek, and thought, *Maybe someday, when Lucy is grown, she will have the right to vote just like men.*

Suzanne came to stand next to me and we hugged. "The day we have waited for!" she said with a smile. "Now, please God, let the war be over soon."

I nodded. It was a happy day, but we were still at war, our country still divided and soldiers still being slaughtered. West Virginia had been admitted into the Union as a free state, but not everyone within its borders was free. Children of slaves born in West Virginia after July 4 would be born free. Slaves less than ten years old would not have their freedom until they turned twenty-one; those between the ages of ten and twenty-one would have to wait until age twenty-five. And no slave from outside of the new state would be allowed to come to West Virginia and live here permanently.

We still had a long way to go before every American citizen would be treated equally in the eyes of the law. There would certainly be pressure on, if not outright persecution of, Confederate West Virginians under the new government. Legislators were already drafting bills that would bar those sworn to CSA loyalty from voting. Yes indeed, we still had a long road ahead of us.

But as I looked at my dear friend and then at my loving husband and children, my heart swelled in my chest. We had each other. We had friendship and family. We loved God and one another. And that love would see us through the worst of times. That's what I believed.

Epilogue

Caroline lived to see the end of the Civil War but not long enough to see her children grow to adulthood. Her fourth child and third son, Bloomfield, was born in 1864, and her fifth, a son named Rufus, was just a baby when Caroline died on October 15, 1867, just days before Adam's 12th birthday. Lucy died ten days after her mother.

Adam—his children and grandchildren referred to him as Adam Clark—became a farmer, as did his brother William. Bloomfield became a merchant and Rufus a Methodist minister.

Both Caroline and Lucy contracted a disease that was then called flux. We now call it dysentery, and it can be caused by a variety of infections. Records indicate that more than 80,000 soldiers died of flux during the Civil War.

As many men did in those days, Frank remarried and raised more children with his second wife Albina. Their names were Squire, Bedford, Fannie, Martha, Mary Ann, Alice, and Margaret.

How I found out about Caroline

My grandmother Minnie Velma Backus died in the spring of 1993 in Charleston, West Virginia. After her passing and my mother's death the following year, I sifted through boxes of Grandma's keepsakes. Among her treasures was a letter, dated 1854, that was written to her grandmother Caroline.

It is a love letter, written in ink on delicate paper. The penmanship is exquisite—beautiful loops of calligraphy—and the words are elegant and respectful. In it, the letter writer expresses his "ardent desire to form an acquaintance" with her. *Her.* Caroline, my great-great-grandmother.

Curiously, though, the name signed at the bottom of the letter was not that of my great-great-grandfather Benjamin Franklin Backus. The writer was Nathan Hanna of Peter's Creek, Nicholas County, Virginia. Caroline lived at that time on a mountain in Nicholas County. Panther Mountain.

How was it, then, that this letter from a suitor who ultimately did not win her heart and become her husband was saved for 150-plus years? Caroline must have kept it, as did her son Adam Clark. The letter then came into my grandma's possession. And now I have the letter, which is mostly intact. A tear in the paper appears to have cut off only one or two words.

Why save a letter from this man? Who was he, and why was he important to Caroline and her offspring?

Thus began my search for answers. That search took me to libraries at West Virginia University in Morgantown, the West Virginia State Archives in Charleston, and the Library of Virginia in Richmond. I came to know quite a bit about Caroline's life. I found out that she was one of eleven children and she and her family were Methodist Episcopalians. Her father, a successful farmer and landowner, was a lay minister, and her home was a stopping place for the traveling pastors of early nineteenth-century Nicholas County, Virginia. Her family owned many books; some say theirs was the largest private library in the community.

152

The Groses and their friends and extended family built the first church building in Nicholas County in 1810. A rebuilt Bethel Church still stands along WV State Route 129 near the location of the first church and the camp meeting grounds on Laurel Creek. Most Western Virginia Methodist Episcopalians of that era–the Groses and Backuses included—were against slavery because it violated their religious beliefs. They very naturally aligned with nineteenth-century abolitionists. Groses and Backuses served in Union militias and regiments during the Civil War.

I looked further into my cousin Kitty Clark Harter Palausky's meticulous genealogy research (her middle name comes from Adam Clark's) and bought a subscription to Ancestry.com. I scoured digitized census records, vital statistics, letters and diaries, newspapers and books to find hints about Caroline—how she dressed, what she ate, how she prayed, what she read, whom she admired, her politics and social views.

This book is a composite of her personal history and the histories of Virginia, West Virginia, the United States, and the Methodist Episcopal Church between 1844 and 1863. Some parts of *Panther Mountain* actually happened and some are fictionalized, based on what I know about Caroline's character and what I believe she would have done in certain situations.

What do I know about Nathan Hanna, the suitor and letter writer? I don't have a full picture. There were multiple men named Nathan Hanna who lived in that part of Virginia during the book's time period. I could not pin down exact information on who this particular man was except for where he lived. The suitor named Nathan Hanna in this book is a composite character. According to the records I've found, more than one Nathan Hanna served in the Confederate Army during the Civil War.

Despite the possibility that the Hannas and other families of Panther Mountain might have been on opposite sides during the war, however, the letter survived. And so did the Union.

Acknowledgements

This book would not have been written had my grandmother, Minnie Velma Backus (1898-1993) not saved the letter that Nathan Hanna wrote to Caroline Grose in 1854. Presumably, my great-grandfather Adam Clark Backus saved the letter before that. I owe my "grands" a debt of gratitude for holding onto this wonderful piece of history.

My cousin Kitty Harter Parkins Palausky laid our genealogy groundwork years ago and has been instrumental in helping me find out more about the Groses and Backhouses/Backuses. I am also grateful that she has kept in touch with our extended family and even organized a couple of family reunions in the 1990s. Kitty's daughter, my cousin Jennifer Spriggel, helped with those as well and has been my close buddy and encourager since we grew up together in Spencer, WV.

I am grateful to *Panther Mountain: Caroline's Story* 's early readers, including my children Patrick and Dana Tuohey ("Mom, you have to write it in first person!"); my husband Chris; my sister Lisa Perry Nazzaro; BFF since kindergarten Sara Johe Busse; BFF since college Laura Leeson Wright; and longtime friend Ed Bazel.

Research into the history of ante- and post-bellum Virginia/West Virginia required me to hit the road several times. I traveled to Morgantown twice to comb through West Virginia University's West Virginia and Regional History Collection. I found a grainy, photocopied photograph of my great-great-great-grandparents William and Susan Grose (Caroline's parents)in the Library of Virginia archives in Richmond, VA. In West Virginia's state capital, my hometown of Charleston, I found further evidence of my ancestors' 19th century lives. On each of these trips, I was accompanied and cheered on by my dear friend and travel buddy Suzanne Lysak, whose patience and kind company were essential to my historical digging.

I would also like to thank the archive and library staffs at all three of those fine institutions, including Debra Basham and Denise Ferguson at West Virginia Archives and History in Charleston, and Christy Venham and Catherine Rakowski at WVU's West Virginia and Regional History Collection in Morgantown.

Daughter Dana was along on the Richmond trip as well, and good-naturedly waited while I pored over a sheaf of Grose/Legg family historical papers. My cousin Jane Backus Skeldon met me in Summersville in June 2014 and we visited the Nicholas County Historical Museum and the county courthouse, where we found Caroline and Frank's original marriage certificate. Also on that trip, historical society member Thomas King kindly knocked on doors, queried local residents and endured a thrill ride in my Hyundai Sonata up a rutted, roadless forest path in search of the Grose family cemetery (we didn't find it but will try again sometime).

Friends and fellow writers/journalists who deserve thanks for their encouragement include Soo Yeon Hong, Aileen Gallagher, Amy Shook and Simon Perez, Dona Hayes, Frank and Donna Currier, and Charlotte Grimes.

On one particular Virginia trip, I met Tamera Mams, a gifted graphic designer who agreed to design *Panther Mountain's* cover. I am so glad we had the chance to work together. Also, I tip my hat to *Panther Mountain's* editor, Sarah Andrews of

Sundragon Editing. Her sharp eye and precision made the book better, clearer and more accurate.

I am also indebted to my distant cousin Pam Backus, whom I connected with via MyFamily.com. Pam provided me with vital information about the Backhouse/Backus family, scanning and emailing me pages from Nicholas County history books.

Most of all, I thank Chris, Dana and Patrick for their love, encouragement, great senses of humor and honest feedback. I have hit the jackpot in the family lottery, thanks be to God.

Bibliography

Books

Bowen, Elias. *Slavery in the Methodist Episcopal Church*. Auburn, NY: William J. Moses, 1859. Google Books e-book. http://books.google.com/books/about/Slavery_in_the_Methodist_Episcopal_Churc.html?id=MVsSAAAAIAAJ.

Brown, William Griffee. *Bethel Church: Oldest Church in Nicholas County*. Nicholas County, 1952.

Brown, William Griffee. *History of Nicholas County, West Virginia*. Nicholas County, WV: Higginson, 1954.

Callahan, James Morton. *Semi-Centennial History of West Virginia*. Semi-Centennial Commission of West Virginia, 1913. E-book from Hathi Trust Digital Library. http://babel.hathitrust.org/cgi/pt?id=pst.000020054939;view=1up;seq=11.

Campbell, Edward. *Nicholas County, (West) Virginia, Records of the Pioneers, 1818–1860*. Upper Glade, WV: Webster County Historical Society, 1985.

Conser, S. L. M. *Virginia After the War: An Account of Three Years' Experience in Reorganizing the Methodist Episcopal Church in Virginia at the Close of the Civil War*. Indianapolis: Baker-Randolph, 1891. E-book. Internet Archive. http://archive.org/stream/virginiaafterwa00consgoog#page/n4/mode/2up.

De Vinné, Daniel. *The Methodist Episcopal Church and Slavery: A Historical Survey of the Relation of the Early Methodists to Slavery*. New York: Francis Hart, 1857. http://archive.org/stream/methodistepiscop00devi#page/n3/mode/2up.

Emmick, David J. *The Amick Partisan Rangers*. iUniverse, 2007. http://bit.ly/1ANIK6I.

Emmick, David. J. *Defending the Wilderness*. Issaquah, WA: Flying A Books, 2007. http://bit.ly/1Fur0da.

Hymnal of the Methodist Episcopal Church. New York: Nelson & Phillips; Cincinnati: Hitchcock & Walden, 1878. E-book. Internet Archive. https://archive.org/stream/hymnalmethodist08churgoog#page/n4/mode/2up.

Lee, Luther, and E. Smith. *The Debates of the General Conference of the M.E. Church, May 1844*. New York: O. Scott, 1845. Published for the Wesleyan Methodist Connection of America. E-book. Internet Archive. https://archive.org/stream/debatesgeneralc00amergoog#page/n18/mode/2up.

Legg, A. J. *A History of Panther Mountain Community*. Morgantown, WV: Agricultural Extension Division, 1930. Reproduced online on West Virginia Archives and History website. http://www.wvculture.org/history/agrext/panther.html.

Nicholas County Historical and Genealogical Society. *Nicholas County History*. Summersville, WV: 1985.

Nicholas County Historical and Genealogical Society. *Nicholas County, WV Heritage 2000*. Summersville, WV: 1985.

Reger, David B. *West Virginia Geological Survey*. Wheeling, WV: Wheeling News, 1921. E-book. Hathi Trust Digital Library. http://babel.hathitrust.org/cgi/pt?id=uc1.b3840864;view=1up;seq=10

Savory's Compendium of Domestic Medicine: and Companion to the Medicine Chest. Excerpted on Medical Home Remedies website. http://www.doctortreatments.com/19th-century-medicines-healing-drugs-chemicals-herbs.html

Scott, Robert N. *War of the Rebellion: A Compilation of the Official Records of the Union and Confederate Armies*. Series 1, vol. 5. Washington, DC: Government Printing Office, 1881. E-book, Cornell University Library, 1995. http://ebooks.library.cornell.edu/m/moawar/text/waro0005.txt ÷

Sherman, William Tecumseh. *General W. T. Sherman as College President: A Collection of Letters*. Vol. 1. Collected and edited by Walter L. Fleming. Cleveland, OH: Arthur H. Clark, 1912. Google Books e-book. http://bit.ly/1Fqpg3D.

US Congress. *Report of the Joint Committee on the Conduct of the War*, 38th Cong., 2d sess. Washington, DC: Government Printing Office, 1865. E-book. Internet Archive. https://archive.org/details/cu31924096461599.

Wilder, Theodore. *The History of Company C, Seventh Regiment, O.V.I.* Oberlin, OH: J.B.T. Marsh, 1866. E-book. Internet Archive. https://archive.org/details/historyofcompany00wild.

Wilson, Lawrence. *Itinerary of the Seventh Ohio Volunteer Infantry, 1861–1864*. New York, NY, and Washington, DC: Neale, 1907. E-book. Internet Archive. https://archive.org/details/itineraryofseven00wils.

Young, John H. *Our Deportment; or the Manners, Conduct and Dress of the Most Refined Society*. Springfield, MA: W.C. King & Co., 1879 and 1882). E-book. Internet Archive, https://archive.org/stream/ourdeportmentor01youngoog#page/n10/mode/2up.

Dissertations and Theses

Foulds, Matthew. "Enemies of the State: Methodists, Secession and the Civil War in West Virginia, 1845–1872." PhD diss., Ohio State University, 2012. OhioLINK. https://etd.ohiolink.edu/!etd.send_file?accession=osu1337031505&disposition=inline.

Sweet, William Warren. "The Methodist Episcopal Church and the Civil War." PhD thesis, University of Pennsylvania, 1912. Internet Archive. https://archive.org/details/methodistchurch00sweerich.

Articles and Blog Posts

"American Civil War Recipes: Union Hardtack and Confederate Johnnie Cakes." *AmericanCivilWar.com*. *http://americancivilwar.com/tcwn/civil_war/civil_war_cooking.html*.

"An Attack upon Summersville, Virginia" (letter to the *Richmond Examiner*, Wednesday, July 30, 1862). *NYTimes.com*. http://www.nytimes.com/1862/08/07/news/an-attack-upon-summersville-va.html.

AzRA Historical Resources and AzRA Re-Enactors Association/USHist. *American Civil War Ladies' Clothing*. http://www.ushist.com/american_civil-war_ladies_clothing_f.shtml.

Bibb, Henry. "Slavery Under Ideal Conditions." Condensed excerpt from *Narrative of the Life and Adventures of an American Slave*, 1849. *Christian History* website, April 1, 1999. http://www.christianitytoday.com/ch/1999/issue62/62h023.html.

"Biography of Martin M. Andrews (1839–1925)." *Bay-Journal*, 1905. http://bay-journal.com/bay/1he/writings/andrews-martin-m.html.

Burke, Henry. "The Mason-Dixon Line, Part VII—Aunt Jenny." *The River Jordan* (blog), May 24, 2011. http://henryrburke.blogspot.com/2011/05/along-mason-dixon-line-part-vii.html.

Campbell, Archibald W. "There Is No Affinity between Eastern and Western Virginia" (extract from an editorial, *Wheeling Daily Intelligencer*, December 25, 1860). Published in *Union or Secession: Virginians Decide*, Virginia Memory Online Classroom, Library of Virginia. http://www.virginiamemory.com/online_classroom/union_or_s ecession/doc/wheelingintelligencer_1860_12_25.

Cantrell, Elaine. "Antebellum and Civil War Weddings" Hope. Dreams. Life... Love (blog), July 10, 2009. http://elainepcantrell.blogspot.com/2009/07/antebellum-and-civil-war-weddings.html.

Carlile, John Snyder. "We Know Our Rights and Dare Maintain Them" (excerpts from address "To the People of North Western Virginia," *Wheeling Daily Intelligencer*, May 21, 1861). Published in *Union or Secession: Virginians Decide*, Virginia Memory Online Classroom, Library of Virginia. http://www.virginiamemory.com/online_classroom/union_or_s ecession/doc/wheelingintelligencer_1861_05_21.

"Civil War Era Slang and Terms: A Writer's Guide for the American Civil War." *RootsWeb*. http://freepages.genealogy.rootsweb.ancestry.com/~poindexte rfamily/CivilWar.html.

Costa, Tom. *The Geography of Slavery in Virginia*. University of Virginia at Wise Library website. http://www2.vcdh.virginia.edu/gos/.

"Courtship Rituals." *The American Wedding: Courtship and Marriage Rituals, 1889–1929*. Trail End State Historic Site (blog), August-December 1996. http://www.trailend.co/courtship.html.

163

"The Day We Celebrate" (editorial). *Wheeling Daily Intelligencer*, June 20, 1863. Included in the online exhibit *A State of Convenience: The Creation of West Virginia*. http://www.wvculture.org/history/statehood/daywecelebrate. html.

Dent, Marshall Mortimer. "Prepare for a Separation" (excerpts from Monongalia County convention delegate reports, March 16 and March 23, 1861, *Virginia Weekly Star,* Morgantown, VA, reprinted in the *Richmond Enquirer*, March 26, 1861). Published in *Union or Secession: Virginians Decide*, Virginia Memory Online Classroom, Library of Virginia. http://www.virginiamemory.com/online_classroom/union_or_s ecession/doc/richmondenquirer_1861_03_26.

Donegan, Richard. "7th Ohio Volunteers at Kessler's Cross Lanes." *Oberlin Heritage Center* website. http://www.oberlinheritagecenter.org/researchlearn/kesslers.

Donnelly, Shirley. "Lots of Things Happened in Nicholas." *Beckley Post-Herald*, June 5, 1969, p. 4. Archived in West Virginia Division of Culture and History Library, Charleston, WV.

Emmerth, Barbara Louise. "Slavery in Present West Virginia in 1860." *West Virginia History* **21, no. 4 (July 1960): 275–77.** http://www.wvculture.org/history/journal_wvh/wvh21–1.html.

"Female Education, December 1830." Article reprinted from *Mrs. Ware's Magazine*, *Godey's Lady's Book*, December 1830, posted on *Accessible Archives* (blog), December 3, 2012. http://www.accessible-archives.com/2012/12/female-education-december-1830/.

Frey, Robert L. "Methodists." *e-WV/The West Virginia Encyclopedia*. http://www.wvencyclopedia.org/articles/1768.

Gorra, Michael. "The Hinge of War: Michael Gorra on the Civil War's Turning Point." *The Daily Beast*, May 13, 2013. http://www.thedailybeast.com/articles/2013/05/13/the-hinge-of-war-michael-gorra-on-the-civil-war-s-turning-point.html.

Gray, Beverly. "The Underground Railroad in Southern Ohio." *The African American Experience in Southern Ohio* (blog), 1997. http://www.angelfire.com/oh/chillicothe/ugrr.html.

Hanna, Margaret. "Early Border History and Genealogical Notes of Prominent Border Families." Reprinted from the *Kanawha Gazette,* December 27, 1887, and the *Staunton Spectator,* January 11, 1888. Transcribed by Gladys Lavender for Greenbrier County, West Virginia History and *Genealogy Trails* website. http://genealogytrails.com/wva/greenbrier/index.html.

"History of Slavery in West Virginia: Underground Railroad." *Serving History* (website). Last modified March 3, 2015. http://www.servinghistory.com/topics/History_of_slavery_in_West_Virginia::sub::Underground_Railroad.

Kansas Historical Society. "Slave Shackle." *Kansapedia*. http://www.kshs.org/kansapedia/slave-shackle/18726.

Library of Congress. "15th Amendment to the Constitution." *Primary Documents in American History* (web guide). http://www.loc.gov/rr/program/bib/ourdocs/15thamendment.html.

MacLean, Maggie. "Nancy Hart Douglas: Confederate Spy and Guerilla Fighter." *Civil War Women* (blog), November 30, 2007. http://civilwarwomenblog.com/nancy-hart-douglas/.

"Marriages of Nicholas County, Virginia, 1818–1861." West Virginia Regional and History Collection Center, West Virginia University, Morgantown.

Meder-Dempsey, Cathy. "James Sims (1754–1845): Pioneer of Nicholas County, WV." *Opening Doors in Brick Walls* (blog), August 25, 2013. https://openingdoorsinbrickwalls.wordpress.com/2013/08/25/james-sims-1754–1845-pioneer-of-nicholas-county-west-virginia/.

"Methodist History: A History of the Denominations Which Form the Heritage of the United Methodist Church in the United States." Boston University School of Theology Library website. http://www.bu.edu/sthlibrary/library-research-guides/methodism/methodist-history/.

Miller, Gary L. "*Historical Natural History: Insects and the Civil War.*" *American Entomologist 43:227–245,* 1997. Reprinted and adapted. http://entomology.montana.edu/historybug/civilwar2/flies.htm.

Mock, Rita Juanita. "Nothing but Crows and Methodist Preachers: A Study in the Saddle of Circuit Riding Preachers." *Songs of Creation* website. http://www.angelfire.com/fl4/HisBeauty/pages/circuitriders.html.

National Park Service. "A Timeline of Gauley River History." http://www.nps.gov/gari/learn/historyculture/a-timeline-of-gauley-river-history.htm.

O'Connor, Bob. "The Underground Railroad in West Virginia." *Examiner.com*, May 30, 2012. http://www.examiner.com/article/the-underground-railroad-west-virginia.

Scholastic. "Myths of the Underground Railroad." Part of online interactive teacher's guide *The Underground Railroad: Escape from Slavery*. http://teacher.scholastic.com/activities/bhistory/underground railroad/myths.htm.

Schwartz, Marcie. "Children in the Civil War, on the Homefront, on the Battlefield." *Civil War Trust* website. http://www.civilwar.org/education/history/children-in-the-civil-war/.

Scott, Eugene L. "Sam Black, Famed Methodist Circuit Rider, Left a Landmark: He Had Trouble with the Yankee Soldiers and a Few Drunks at 'Hells Half Acre.'" *Beckley Post-Herald*, April 8, 1946. Article transcribed and reprinted on *USGENWEB Greenbrier County, WV*, by Al Zopp, June 19, 1998. http://files.usgwarchives.net/wv/greenbrier/newspapers/samblack.txt.

Shaffer, Donald R. "The 20 Negro Law and Emancipation." *Civil War Emancipation* (blog), October 11, 2012. https://cwemancipation.wordpress.com/2012/10/11/the-20-negro-law-and-emancipation/.

"Shall We Have a New State?" (editorial). *Wheeling Daily Intelligencer*, October 21, 1861. http://chroniclingamerica.loc.gov/lccn/sn84026845/1861–10–21/ed-1/seq-2/.

"Slave Catchers." *US Slave* (blog), May 2, 2011. http://usslave.blogspot.com/2011/05/slave-catchers.html.

Steelhammer, Rick. "Civil War at 150: Egos Led the Way in W.Va.'s Battle of Carnifex Ferry." *Charleston Gazette/wvgazette.com*, September 9, 2011, http://www.wvgazette.com/News/201109091843.

Sutherland, Daniel E. "Guerrilla Warfare in Virginia during the Civil War." *Encyclopedia Virginia*. http://www.encyclopediavirginia.org/guerrilla_warfare_in_virginia_during_the_civil_war#start_entry.

"The Underground Railroad, c. 1780–1862." WGBH/PBS Online. http://www.pbs.org/wgbh/aia/part4/4p2944.html.

"Virginia V. West Virginia." *The American Journal of International Law* 5 (April 1, 1911). JSTOR via Internet Archive. https://archive.org/details/jstor-2186732.

"Virginia; The Restored Government of Virginia—History of the New State of Things." Unattributed letter to the editor of *The New York Times*, Wednesday, June 22, 1864. http://www.nytimes.com/1864/06/26/news/virginia-the-restored-government-of-virginia-history-of-the-new-state-of-things.html?pagewanted=1.

Williams, Preston. "West Virginia: The State That Said No." *Washington Post*, April 12, 2011.
http://www.washingtonpost.com/sports/west-virginia-the-state-that-said-no/2011/03/30/AFLxJrQD_story.html.

Documents

"1850 Census: Instructions to Marshals and Assistant Marshals."
Minnesota Population Center, University of Minnesota
Integrated Public Use Microdata Series (IPUMS USA).
https://usa.ipums.org/usa/voliii/inst1850.shtml.

Blair, Jacob Beeson. Letter to Waitman T. Willey. Published in the
Wheeling Daily Intelligencer, January 22, 1876.
http://www.wvculture.org/history/statehood/blairjb03.html.

Constitution of the State of West Virginia. November 26, 1861. Digitized
by National Archives, Center for Legislative Archives.
http://www.archives.gov/legislative/features/west-virginia/constitution.html.

"Kanawha Salines Bills of Lading Book (April 27, 1850–May 15, 1882)."
PDF. University of Missouri—St. Louis Pott Library Special
Collections. http://www.umsl.edu/mercantile/collections/pott-library-special-collections/assets/pdf/kanawha%20salines.pdf.

Library of Virginia. "How Virginia Convention Delegates Voted on
Secession, April 4 and April 17, 1861, and Whether They Signed
a Copy of the Ordinance of Secession." PDF.
http://www.virginiamemory.com/docs/votes_on_secession.pdf.

McKinley, William. Letter to W. K. Miller, August 11, 1861, Camp at
   Weston, VA. *Civil War Notebook* (blog), March 7, 2014.
   http://civilwarnotebook.blogspot.com/2014/03/private-william-
   mckinley-to-w-k-miller.html.

"To the Legislature of Virginia" (petition from residents of Nicholas
   County, VA, on behalf of Isaac Sims). December 9, 1836. Petition
   11683632, Race and Slavery Petitions Project, Digital Library on
   American Slavery, University of North Carolina at Greensboro.
   https://library.uncg.edu/slavery/petitions/details.aspx?pid=273
   7.

Databases and Collections

Accessible Archives. *Godey's Lady's Book* Collection.
   http://www.accessible-archives.com/collections/godeys-ladys-
   book/.

American Memory. Library of Congress.
   http://memory.loc.gov/ammem/index.html.

America Singing: Nineteenth-Century Song Sheets. Library of Congress,
   Rare Book and Special Collections Division.
   http://memory.loc.gov/ammem/amsshtml/amsshome.html.

Celebrating West Virginia Statehood, June 20, 1863. National Archives,
   Center for Legislative Archives.
   http://www.archives.gov/legislative/features/west-virginia/.

Chronicling America: Historic American Newspapers. Library of
   Congress. http://chroniclingamerica.loc.gov/.

Circuit Rider Database. Auglaize County, OH, Genealogy Page. http://ohauglaize.ancestralsites.com/index1.htm.

Dyer, Frederick H. *Compendium of the War of the Rebellion: Regimental Histories*. Perseus Digital Library, Tufts University. http://www.perseus.tufts.edu/hopper/text?doc=Perseus%3Atext%3A2001.05.0146.

History Engine. University of Richmond. http://historyengine.richmond.edu/pages/home.

"Kessler's Cross Lanes." CWSAC Battle Summaries. http://www.nps.gov/abpp/battles/wv004.htm.

Tubb, Benjamin Robert. *American Civil War Music (1861–1865)* (website). http://www.pdmusic.org/civilwar2.html.

Virginia Secession Convention. University of Richmond. http://collections.richmond.edu/secession/.

Visualizing Emancipation. University of Richmond. http://dsl.richmond.edu/emancipation/#event/26379.

West Virginia Memory Project. West Virginia Division of Culture and History. http://www.wvculture.org/history/wvmemory/index.html.

Genealogical Archival Material

Ancestry.com. Source documents and images, Backus Family Tree.

Bennett, Robert G. (compiler). *Genealogy Research Records* (notebooks of genealogy records regarding the Bennett family of Nicholas

County, WV, inclusive dates 1873–2009). West Virginia and Regional History Center, West Virginia University Library.

FamilySearch. "African-Americans." Bath County, Virginia, Genealogy Resources. https://familysearch.org/learn/wiki/en/Bath_County,_Virginia#African_Americans.

"Inventory of the Debts Due the Estate of M. J. Landcraft." *West Virginia Will Book, volume 001, 1832–1866.* Digitized by *FamilySearch* at *West Virginia Will Books, 1756–1971.* http://bit.ly/1SWhkS1.

Meder-Dempsey, Cathy. "Opening Doors in Brick Walls" (genealogical information on Isaac Sims). *RootsWeb.* http://wc.rootsweb.ancestry.com/cgi-bin/igm.cgi?op=GET&db=meder-dempsey&id=I36671.

Popp, Tony. Genealogical information on the Grose family. *Genealogy.com.* http://www.genealogy.com/forum/surnames/topics/grose/74/.

Snowden, Thelma Legg. *Panther Mountain Pioneers* (March 1988) (copy of typewritten genealogical notes and photo concerning the following pioneer families of Nicholas and Monroe counties, W.Va.: Alderson, Drennen, Dunbar, Grose, Halstead, Hull, Johnson, Koontz, Legg, Lemasters, Lutz, Mason, McClung, McCoy, Morris, Nutter, Rader, Ramsey, Renick, Walker, and Wiseman). Library of Virginia Archives, Richmond, VA.

For more links to *Panther Mountain: Caroline's Story*'s historical resources, please visit www.panthermt.com

55811331R00097

Made in the USA
Charleston, SC
06 May 2016